The Crowded Darkness

BY THE SAME AUTHOR

The Five Lives of Ben Hecht
Gold Diggers of 1929
The Blue Notebook
Variorum: New Poems and Old 1965-1985
Moving Towards the Vertical Horizon
Rites of Alienation
The Gold Crusades: A Social History of Gold Rushes 1849–1929
A George Woodcock Reader (editor)
Documents in Canadian Art (editor)
Documents in Canadian Film (editor)

The Crowded Darkness

DOUGLAS FETHERLING

Quarry Press
& Subway Books

CANADIAN CATALOGUING IN PUBLICATION DATA

Fetherling, Douglas, 1949–
The Crowded Darkness

Includes index.
ISBN 0-919627-13-7
1. Motion pictures — United States — Reviews.
I. Title
PN1995.F48 1988   791.43'75'0973   C88-090285-X

Design & imaging by ECW Production Services, Sydenham, Ontario.
Printed by Hignell Printing Limited, Winnipeg, Manitoba.
Co-published by Quarry Press, Inc., Kingston, Ontario
and Subway Books Ltd., Toronto, Ontario.
Distributed by University of Toronto Press,
5201 Dufferin Street, Downsview, Ontario M3H 5T8

Contents

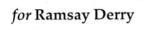

for Ramsay Derry

Preface

This book is selected largely from the film column I conducted in the venerable *Canadian Forum* for several years in the 1970s. I was commenting quite a bit on film for various publications (and two or three articles from those other sources are also included here) and was accustomed to having little or no attention paid to what I wrote. Certainly I wasn't expecting much response from what would appear in the *Forum*. Despite its motto "An Independent Journal of Opinion and the Arts," the *Forum* is usually an independent journal of only one or the other, depending on its editor at any given moment.

At the time of which I speak, the thrust was clearly political, not cultural. Even during its alternating periods as an arts organ, it has tended to view popular culture disdainfully when not ignoring it altogether. When, in an uncharacteristic move, it commissioned a readership survey, the constituency of the film column was found to be predictably small. Yet however few they might have been, the readers were amazingly communicative. Letters would arrive crediting me with sophistry, snobbery, illiteracy, homosexuality, even artistry. Many of these letters were signed. And many more people telephoned or came up to me at parties and the like than put their thoughts on paper. In a couple decades of contributing to magazines, I have never received more comment nor seen comment continue so long. Even now I frequently hear what follows in these pages remarked on, pro or con.

The reaction was pleasing but somewhat disconcerting because the copy was usually written weeks after seeing the film and in the last hour or so before the absolutely final deadline and only as a break between other types of scribbling. Yet the emotions aroused were hardly inexplicable. Although there were columns on important new Canadian releases (a couple of which are included here; others are in a volume of mine entitled *The Blue Notebook*), and although I occasionally dealt with European ones, the preponderance of space was usually given over to Hollywood products. American movies in what seems that remote time had not yet deteriorated into the psychotic violence and pathological patriotism that make them unwatchable today, but were nonetheless sufficiently diseased to serve as good lecture topics. Therefore the column contained, as a rule, more social criticism than film criticism. Hence, I hope, the clinical anti-pro-Americanism that so enraged or tickled others at the time. It is a quality that seems to me sufficient reason to republish these jottings, with minor alterations.

I see that in one of these reviews from the era of Vietnam and Watergate I refer to "the crowded darkness" in which a certain actor's beginnings appear lost. At this remove, the phrase seems more telling than it did at the time. The crowded darkness of the cinema itself. The crowded darkness of history, with which many of the pieces appear to be grappling so crudely. The crowded darkness of the empire that is the real subject of what follows.

The End of Ricco

I

Bob Wiedrich, a columnist with the Chicago *Tribune*, recently published a piece in that paper's Sunday magazine about the city's old-time gang bosses, a species almost extinct. The article made the obvious point that the current crime nabobs in the Athens of Corruption are either nouveaux riches blacks or hoodlums who entered the business when very young in the 1930s at the latest. The story focused on the most notable exception, Tony Accardo, who is perhaps the last of the old Sicilian czars still active there. His story is very sad. The tone and sweep of his biography parallel and throw light on *Godfather Part II*, the final instalment of Francis Ford Coppola's masterpiece.

Depending upon which source one uses, Accardo was born either in Chicago or in the old country, seventy years ago this April. In any case, he was close enough to the steerage so that no one has faulted his Italian. His first arrests were in 1922. His first recorded employment was sitting outside Al Capone's suite in the Metropole Hotel with a Thompson gun — a Chicago typewriter, if you will — across his lap. He's thought by some to have had some hand in the St. Valentine's Day massacre. To a U.S. gangster this is what having been at the storming of the Winter Palace is to a Russian patriot.

Accardo ascended to real power in 1947 after Capone's heir presumptive, Frank (The Enforcer) Nitti, died either by his own hand or by someone else's masquerading as his own. He's alive still, an infirm old character on the North Shore, surrounded by John Dean-type lawyers who think Capone is a myth from another century. The empire is crumbling and he knows it. He himself is dying and he knows this too. He's conceivably the last man left breathing who could answer with certainty the fifty-year-old questions "Who killed Jake Lingle and why?" and "What really happened to McSwiggin?" He knows the answers. He's aware that *we* know that he knows them. And still he's not saying. This raises the philosophical point of what is truth, what is history, once the survivors are gone, the facts are lost forever and even the atmosphere has vanished? It's a question Coppola has had to wrestle with in the making of this film.

Chronologically speaking, *The Godfather Part II* (let's call it Film Two) is not only the second part of the story. What it is really is the beginning and ending of a noble American epic in which the original movie (Film One) formed the middle. Film Two relates the story of Michael Corleone (Al Pacino), who became head of the family upon the death, among the sunflower stalks and tomato plants, of his father Tony Corleone (Marlon Brando). In this film, the continued rise of Pacino is intercut with the story, hitherto unseen, of his father's early years on both sides of the Atlantic. In several unsubtle but finely realized ways, the two movies taken together tell the moral story of America in this century, even up to the uncertainty of the present time.

Many members of the fabled first generation of Chicago gangsters, from whom virtually all the cinema stereotypes are derived, were dead or dying by the time audiences became interested in them. They had been, in the main, ward heelers in the ethnic communities with a tradition of extortion behind them and the promise of the New World in front. For some, the first contact with Anglo-Saxon business practices came when they were hired to beat up opposing thugs in the great newspaper circulation wars of 1907-

2

12. Already tough, they soon became wise. They knew a good thing when the saw it in the Volstead Act of 1919 and so established themselves as beer barons. The smarter, more powerful ones employed lesser ones, veterans home from the Great War with nothing but a knowledge of the Lewis machine gun, and started killing off their rivals. It was free enterprise in microcosm. Silent films were just beginning to offer Americans the vicarious kick of seeing themselves thus idealised when in the late 1920s the real thing began to fade, or at least to change.

The worship of material success in America (not to say violence) has always gone hand-in-hand with the idea that it's somehow demoralising. The Hays Office of the 1930s was only reflecting the attitudes of the theatre-goers by demanding that gangsters in such early talkies as *Scarface, Public Enemy,* and *Little Caesar* meet justice in the last scenes. The people who wrote these films, old police reporters with ambivalent feelings about the real gangsters, knew better but deferred to public taste. Later movies made clichés of the truthful elements in such scripts.

There were two reasons for this. The first was that a new generation of screenwriters arose who began writing without having had any real contact with the underworld. This in turn was because, in the transition (abetted by such films) from organised crime to institutionalised crime, the underworld had in fact gone underground. What two generations of box office queues have been left with is the gangster myth, in which Americans have used these last individualists to tell the story of their own value system. Coppola's two movies are the highest embodiment of this genre, brought up to date.

The casts of the two films are largely the same save for the absence here of Brando. In the flashbacks depicting his childhood and immigration his part is filled by a child actor and in those showing his early criminal life by Robert De Niro, who starred in *Mean Streets.* Coppola has tried to resolve the question of philosophical truth by aiming instead for historical typicality. The young Corleone as we see him here is an amalgamation of odds and ends of general truth jazzed up by dramatic (and sometimes unconvincing) speculation.

He was born in 1892 in Calabria, where his father and later his brother and mother were murdered by the Black Hand. At age nine he is shipped off to America to avoid the same fate. That he will make his fortune in the New World is incidental, which is in part

3

perhaps why he succeeds so brilliantly. Coppola's picture of the wave of immigration is painfully nostalgic, as though to point out that only when the flow ceased did the nation begin erecting monuments in granite to its own shortcomings. In showing the shame and the promise of Ellis Island he is making a quite dramatic statement on his own Italian-ness, with all the handicaps and advantages which go along with such ancestral feeling.

Coppola has the young, already raspy-voiced Corleone starting his new life in New York rather than in Chicago or in any of the smaller immigrant centres. He does so to take advantage of the Big Apple as the symbol of America itself, to make it the home of tastemakers and power-mongers it was in fact for more than a century. The scenes of the Mulberry Street area are brilliantly photographed and reminiscent in texture of parts of Bo Widerberg's *Joe Hill*. They are evocative of (in Allen Ginsberg's phrase) "the streets with their pushcarts full of onions and bad music." Yet Coppola doesn't over-sentimentalize as many would do in his position. He could have used panchromatic sweeps, the way a hack would have done. Or he could have used grainy, antiquitous black-and-white, to divorce these characters from himself in time, the way a Bogdanovich would have done. Instead he chose washed-out postcard hues. He knows these were vicious, ignorant people, however much they are a part of us all.

Instinctive ladder climbing and the memory of what happened to his family cause the young Corleone to bump off the neighbourhood extortionist and put himself, socially at least, in the man's place. He becomes the boss of Little Italy. When we last see him he returns for a holiday to his natal village where he receives a hero's welcome. While there, he kills the, by now, doddering, harmless old fool who once murdered a generation and a half of Corleones. What we do not see explained is the ambition or whatever it was that made him keep climbing rather than remain a big fish in a small fetid pond. What we don't see is the drive that created the Godfather from what was potentially just another transitory punk. Or at least we don't see it in Tony Corleone. We see it instead in his son, when the story picks up in the 1950s.

What made Michael take over from his father at the end of Film One and keeps him moving forward in Film Two is his anachronistic sense of duty. Duty as a tradition, something his father seemed to pass on to the boy in his genes as much as by example. Part of the tradition is the belief in the family unit, which Michael sees

4

breaking down. He's a man tormented by the problem of how to maintain the integrity of his traditions without cutting them off from modern society, which would mean an end to everything. He's like a man with a beautiful wife whose beauty he finds most invigorating and unbearable when it's displayed in the company of other men. The other men in this case are infidels who try to betray him to the Kefauver Commission and the old Jewish syndicate brain Hyman Roth (Lee Strasberg), an outsider but an oldtimer and an equal power, with whom truck is onerous but necessary, at least for a time.

Part of the success of the Corleone characters of these films is that they are believable composites. Brando was a little Vito Genovese, a little Joe Bananas, a touch of Luciano, giving the illusion of documentation while summing up a type rather than a set of individuals. The films are more successful at this than Mario Puzo's novel was. The Roth character is different. He's blatantly modelled on one man, Meyer Lansky. Ingredients of the role — such as his ailing health, his attempt to escape prosecution by settling in Israel under the Law of the Return, and his impromptu press conference in Miami following the failure of that attempt — are striking because the TV coverage of these actual events is still fresh in our minds. The difference is that in the film Roth is murdered by Michael Corleone whereas Lansky is still with us. Roth's killing follows his attempt to have Corleone done in at Havana, where Roth has failed (as Lansky did in real life) in a bid to keep Batista in power and erect an empire like that which his partner Bugsy Siegel built in Las Vegas. (In Film One, Siegel was characterized as Moe Green, who was shot in the eye as he lay on a massage table, just as Siegel was shot in the eye in the home of his mistress Virginia Hill.)

Putting the films together and leaving Michael aside for a moment, the story is about Anthony Corleone's boyhood and early rise at about the time of the First World War and about his *Realpolitik* in the late 1930s and the decade after. What's missing is the tale of his swifter, bloodier elevation during Prohibition. The inclusion of this would have made his story too much like most every other gangster picture, something Coppola has avoided, being more interested in the psychology of power than in clichés. Still, Film One, much more than the slower paced Film Two, was a traditional gangster movie, with the requisite number of machine gun snaildrums, sinister black limos and shattered panes of plate glass.

5

Film Two is less violent, less hackneyed and more insightful and satisfying. It's a story about the seemingly necessary abuses of power and of the replacement of the traditional sense of duty (to country, family, whatever) with a sense of duty to happiness, which is the dominant ethical theme of recent American life. Happiness has become a status symbol rather than a quality. Film Two is a movie, set psychologically in the gangster idiom, about the American quest for the perfect tan. It's also one which questions, without drawing conclusions, the apparently decreasing need in our society for literal truth as represented by historical fact. And this brings me back to Tony Accardo.

I once had the eerie experience of seeing Darryl F. Zanuck's *The Longest Day* in the company of a group of men who had waddled ashore on Omaha Beach in 1944. They watched silently and afterward reflected bravely on how in real life the water had been so much deeper and the enemy gunfire so much lower. Similarly, I viewed the premiere of *The Battle of Britain* in the Leicester Square Odeon surrounded by old RAF pilots who seemed shaken by the accuracies and inaccuracies presented in tribute to their work. I would like to have the opportunity of watching Accardo while he watched *The Godfather Part II* for the first time. My guess is that he would be silent and attentive and later, walking out into the sunlit Loop, oddly introspective, at least for a moment. And then — then he wouldn't say a word, ever. Accardo and his kind were the last Old Americans and the first of the New.

February 1975

II

There is a scene in Steve Carter's film *Capone* in which the legendary American crime lord, played this time by Ben Gazzara, tells reporters that he believes gangster films are a bad influence since they cause young people to aspire to be hoodlums instead of president of the United States. In Menahem Golan's film *Lepke* there is an even less subtle scene in which the title character, a New York racketeer of the 1930s and 1940s, shoots it out with rivals in a deserted movie palace while a noisy gangster film is being projected on the screen. These are indications that both films, like recent gangster pictures as a class, are concerned with the difference between the well documented cinema gangster and the less tangible figure on whom the stereotype originally was based. This in turn is part of a larger concern about moral evolution which all of us presently share.

Anyone who makes a gangster film today still runs the risk of being accused of romanticising crime. This applies even to Francis Ford Coppola, whose two gangster pictures are such fine examples of movie manufacturing that they elevated the whole genre to a higher position than it occupied even in the 1930s. The complaint has persisted for almost fifty years even though the reason why anyone should *want* to glamourise gangsters has changed several times.

In the late 1920s and early 1930s gangsters were important to the people as a source of vicarious pleasure, not to say for the actual services they provided in the tippling and gambling areas. One had one's favourite gangster and one repeated with private satisfaction the funny nickname bestowed upon him by the newspapers. It was the time of big dough, and a person admired his or her pet gangster equally for the way in which he had rapidly accumulated his pile and for the tenaciousness with which he hung on to it. Later, during the Depression, the gangster occupied even more the place of the movie star by the lavish and unrealistic lifestyle he maintained even while other people were freezing in soup lines with old funny papers tucked under their shirts.

Eventually prosperity returned and the gangster began to seem corny, especially when men were actually killing other people in the war. Besides, the gangster was a creature of the past. Now there was the racketeer instead, a far less public and therefore more sinister character who, rather than providing beer and a good read,

7

was engaged in some dark activity, we didn't know what. In the middle and late 1930s public attention (rather than Hollywood's) had been focussed on the yokels in the midwest and southwest like Bonnie and Clyde and Dillinger whom people liked to believe had turned mean because they were poor. Hollywood later caught up with these characters as well, and they too soon became hokey.

All this is to say that film audiences long enjoyed gangster movies, at least on a subliminal level, because both they and the films were either romantic or idealistic. Now the motivation is entirely different, and Carter's *Capone*, the latest in a long series of biopix of the swarthy Chicagoan, is a good indication of this. It is a good indication that while our viewpoint on the film gangster has changed, our moral expectation of the real life figure has not kept up with the times.

Surely Capone's story is the great American tragedy. Born in the New York slums, he grew up pugnacious in order to survive. By virtue of this pugnacity he was shipped to Chicago by Johnny Torrio who, as fortune would have it, grew tired and reticent and decided to retire. Thus while still in his early twenties Capone fell heir to a business which he made into an empire by hard slugging and great inventiveness. Judges, senators and governors were coiled around his little finger, and part of the privilege of his position was access to the press. He took advantage of this access for all it was worth but in the process was taken advantage of himself. He became the biggest name in his field but also the biggest target for the jealous hypocrites in public office.

Eventually he was nabbed for failing to pay his income tax (all of it, not just the part that would have gone to the defence budget) and was sent to prison in that less enlightened time for the same act that later would make a heroine of Joan Baez. Freed at last, a man ahead of his rightful time whom the media had used up and discarded, he died of syphilis at forty-eight, an age when most men are just having their first heart attack. Surely if organised crime should ever become an academic subject there will be found here enough meat for the dissertations of an entire generation. Surely, in this unlikely event, one of the first theses would be a study of Capone's film iconography and its relation to our changing standards of behaviour.

Although it was coquettishly denied at the time, Capone was clearly the factual basis for such films as *Little Caesar* in 1930 and *Scarface* two years later. Because the official morality in those days

8

was lagging so far behind the unofficial one, the makers of these and other films found it necessary to disguise their products as exposés of social evils. Thus *Scarface* was subtitled "The Shame of a Nation" and Paul Muni came to grief at the end. Similarly, Edward G. Robinson in *Little Caesar* died in the last frames also, though with more disbelief than contrition, as he uttered the famous line, "Ah, Mother of Mercy! Is this the end of Ricco?" He needn't have worried, of course; it was far from the end, though the way these words would be received was beginning to change.

Throughout the 1930s gangster films limped along in the ways already outlined and then all but disappeared in the 1940s. In the 1958 film *Al Capone* Rod Steiger became the first to play the character by name. His was a Method Capone in theory but a television one in practice. This intense Scarface knew his lines and how to find his mark, and he illustrated nothing so much as the 1950s desire to promote conventionality as a virtue and to rewrite history for this purpose. Two years later in *The Scarface Mob*, a spinoff of *The Untouchables* television series, Neville Brand diverted history even more by portraying an inarticulate tyrannical Capone with a heavy Italian accent, at a time when racial tensions and the perpetual battle between socialism and free enterprise were at their greatest peaks since 1919. Although it lacked the tax evasion and VD elements, the best Capone story was the 1967 film *The St. Valentine's Day Massacre*, starring Jason Robards. It was made in the documentary style and with, by Hollywood standards, meticulous attention to historical fact. It appeared, not coincidentally, at a time when gangsters were becoming a subject of nostalgia as, to some people, the last great robber barons, and, to others, the last great anti-authoritarian individualists.

The St. Valentine's Day Massacre was directed by the eclectic Roger Corman, who is the producer of the present *Capone*, and this helps explain why a piece of the former film was lifted as stock footage for the latter. But what's more interesting is that the author of both scripts is Howard Browne, a China hand among Chicago pulp writers. The choice is interesting because it allows us to see how the same man using the same materials writes differently (perhaps unconsciously so) for the middle 1960s and the middle 1970s.

When the first film was made, people were still ambivalent about the old-time gangsters. We had ceased believing that villains had to die in the last reel but we weren't entirely certain of the gangster's place in society. For the 1970s film, however, we at last have come to terms with the prototype gangster as a basic component of society, like Walter Cronkite or Ralph Nader. Or at least we have come to feel this way when thinking of the past.

As once the unofficial morality was far ahead of the official one, so now the reality of gangsters is slightly ahead of our consciousness of them. We do not laugh at the line in Carter's film about the president of the United States because we think in retrospect that Capone wouldn't have made any worse a president that Lyndon Johnson or Richard Nixon. At least old Al had charisma. We have now come full circle save for one little open space at the top: the awareness (hinted at in Coppola's *Godfather II*) that a gangster could in fact be elected president in the U.S. right now, and that perhaps one already was a few years ago. Bebe Rebozo, it's no exaggeration, could have played in *The Scarface Mob* quite convincingly, and this frightens us. The historical Capone is more pleasing, more entertaining, because we know that, all else he was, he was not a civil servant and that as an anarchist of sorts would never have become one.

In the early 1930s, patrons of gangster films came away from the cinema where a villain had been depicted and went down to the corner speak managed by (as far as they could tell) a glamorous local businessman. Today we come out of *Capone* having seen a glamorous businessman and pick up the newspaper to read that Sam Giancana, a real life Capone veteran, was involved in a Kennedy-CIA plot to bump off Fidel Castro and was himself eliminated when this became known. In the next film about him to appear, Capone will seem a veritable good guy by remaining unchanged while the standards of the audience will have shifted even more. This future epic will have to be subtitled "The Shame of a Government," and only then will there be romanticising of crime.

The newspaper matrixes for Carter's *Capone* have carried the line, "Now, after 45 years the true story can be told." Apparently this refers in part to the fact of Capone's syphilis, which has been public knowledge for years but not film knowledge (Steiger's film alluded to the disease without naming it. That was 1958, remember). But this sentence also apparently refers to the fact that Browne shows Capone to have been betrayed by his lieutenant Frank Nitti — a theory which has been voiced by criminals, crime reporters and coppers for almost as long. By comparison, the ads for Golan's *Lepke*, which stars Tony Curtis, contain likenesses of the cast alongside photographs of the actual crime leaders of the time. Frankly, there is little physical resemblance. But this is fitting since the screen story has little more than a foundation of historical truth, and too little is made of the treachery of J. Edgar Hoover and Walter Winchell, who were equal villains in this matter.

Yet this historical sales angle taken with both films is interesting. It is as though the producers are saying, "Look, folks, this is history. It can't hurt you. These people have been dead for years. They aren't the elected gangsters we read and hear about. They're not even the non-elected gangster friends of these people. It's only a movie, folks. It's safe." This is a fascinating if rather pitiful statement on present-day U.S. internal affairs. One awaits the film that will go one big step further and risk the old audience while supplying a new, though the wait may be in vain. *Godfather III* or some such, were it ever to come to pass, would doubtless be suppressed for reasons of national security.

August 1975

III

There has been much justifiable complaining about the lack of substantial film roles for women. The thrust of the criticism is that there are few believable parts for women in modern dress, a situation that may have a lot to do with natural cycles. Some of the concern, however, has been about the number of parts in general, especially parts calling for some independence of spirit. Sometimes it seems that such anxiety has eclipsed the cinematic past, where conditions were somewhat better. There is something like self-fulfilling prophecy at work here.

That was brought home to me watching two films on television, one from the distant movie past, the other more recent. The films were Frank Capra's *Ladies in Distress* (1930), with Barbara Stanwyck in her third job, and Arthur Penn's *Bonnie and Clyde* (1967). Between the making of the first and the making of the second, a whole category of female character died or was killed off. I refer to the Hollywood gun moll, a more admirable character than the phrase would first suggest. Stanwyck, twenty-two at the time, was a terrific gun moll, full of life, independence and snide remarks, though she was not strictly speaking playing a gun moll but only a gun moll type. Faye Dunaway was, by comparison, a washout because her role as Bonnie Parker did not match the time-honoured notion of how it should be played.

Gun molls were probably the first independent women in movies, or at least the first to impose themselves on the audience by force of frequency and numbers. They were creatures of the very late 1920s at the earliest. Although there are examples in the silent cinema (Feathers McCoy in Josef von Sternberg's *Underworld*), it was only with the talkies that they came into their own. So much depended upon their backtalk and natty repartee. (My own favourite gun moll line: "It's your front teeth you're gambling with, bozo" — circa 1935.)

It was, I believe, the early action talkies, especially the Warner ones and the gangster films in particular, that established the image of the wise-cracking, usually lanky moll. She had a will of her own and, in the end, often led her male companion to destruction. Although she crossed the line into golddigger sometimes, she was always several notches above the mere chorus girl in intelligence and was never sinister in her own right. Examples that come to mind are Joan Blondell, who was quite a moll before moving on to only slightly better things, and the early Myrna Loy. Another is Veronica Lake, who remained consistently mollish. Bette Davis was also a rather good moll when young, before she was typecast as a neurotic.

What made the gun moll different from every other screen stereotype was her relationship with the opposite sex. With weak men, she was contemptuous or condescending. With strong men, she was flippant but never arch or asinine, assertive but not obstreperous, affectionate without being doting. She lived in a male world in hundreds of gangster films, newspaper films and such but on almost equal footing with the male. She was like the male with the violence taken away. There was even the odd picture putting her in the foreground and the male in the background. One thinks of that ripoff of *Public Enemy* entitled *Wife of Public Enemy*.

In her time she was the freest and sexiest creature afoot, even if those qualities were more to be inferred than demonstrated by what was shown on the screen. In *To Have and Have Not*, as Peter Bogdanovich has pointed out in quite another context, one knows by instinct at what point Bacall and Bogart go to bed together, although there is no real evidence of such a thing taking place. Bacall in 1944: now there was a gun moll to be reckoned with.

That the gun moll was first and most importantly a character in gangster films was, it seems to me, because the studios intended her to be recognized by some as a sex symbol but by others as a whore, or at least a slut. She could be both sexy and virtuous, impure and evil only for so long as she was a near criminal or an aider and abettor of criminals. When gangster films lapsed into irrelevance, the gun moll died out, or at least changed a great deal. At one level she became the Hepburnian career woman in the tweed suit and all the variants of same. At another she became Myrna Loy of the *Thin Man* series: possessor of a more urbane raunchiness, of gentility superimposed upon tackiness or perhaps the other way around. With the new wave of gangster films in the 1950s and 1960s — the ones about the Barkers, Bonnie and Clyde, Dillinger — the gun moll reappeared as an actual gun moll. She was more independent than before but this was a concession to social change rather than a herald of it. So it is at present. Not only aren't there many juicy parts for women, there are few if any for women called Roxie, Trix or Feathers McCoy.

December 1977 – January 1978

Carry on Hildy

I

One of the most surprising things about the National Film Board feature *Why Rock the Boat?* comes at the very end as part of the crawl. Among the acknowledgments to those who have helped in some way is one to the Montreal *Gazette*, the paper William Weintraub used as a model for his 1961 novel, on which his script of the same title is loosely based. Although the experience has been ascibed to the defunct *Herald*, it was in fact the *Gazette* that Weintraub worked for briefly in the late 1940s and is satirizing in both book and film. The paper's help is surprising because the *Gazette*, like most other Canadian papers and the Toronto and Montreal dailies in particular, is known by this credo: *We never hold a grudge but we never forget.* And the attack on the *Gazette* in the film is even more biting than the one in the book, being more a caricature and less a traditional satire.

The differences in plot, style and tone between the novel and the movie present a good opportunity for some fiction-film comparative criticism, which is the best new discipline around. The most important of the discrepancies are the changes in tense. The book (pretty light stuff, incidentally) was written with no particular consideration of recent human history. Although Weintraub composed it more than a decade after the fact, the novel could be set with equal ease at the time of the writing or twenty years farther back with the adjustment of a few references. In the film, however, he makes use not of the flat Historical Past Tense but of the Nostalgic Present Tense, which has recently become quite popular.

In the Historical Past, history is represented only by the choice of locations and the choice of costumes for the actors peopling them. Little attention is paid to the accuracy of small details and even less speech. To take an example: in every western made before *True Grit*, the nineteenth-century characters spoke like Barbara Frum and usually dressed like guests at a costume party, so that whole generations have gone to their graves thinking the past was just like the present, only dustier. The filmmaker's intent was merely to tell a story. But in the Nostalgic Present the director has another purpose in mind: to make us squirm with embarrassment over how silly we were back then, just this side of memory's horizon, which is as far as most people's awareness of history extends. This approach is only possible with films set in the past couple of decades and has been a very popular one, as witness the success of films such as *Summer of '42, American Graffiti* — and *Why Rock the Boat?*

When we see twenty-one-year-old reporter Harry Barnes (Stuart Gillard) worrying about the way his virginity sticks to him like flypaper, we shudder at the very recollection and slide lower in our seats. We get the same effect from seeing the way he wastes his emotion on rival reporter Julia Martin (Tiiu Leek), who's a middle class beauty suffering from delusions of radicalism — Cybill Shepherd on her way to becoming Patty Hearst. If in the viewer's real life the virginity was retained a few years longer or disposed of a few years sooner, or if it happened in the 1950s or 1960s instead of in the 1940s, or if the other person in question was even more or somewhat less of a squeaky clean twit, it makes no difference. It's excruciating to watch because it is popular history we can identify with, reinforced by inanimate objects true not to the period but to the very year being recalled; and that — heavy petting, sock hops and pants pegged or baggy — is the stuff of human nature.

15

Still, it is only one approach, and one wonders what part of the attractiveness of *The Apprenticeship of Duddy Kravitz* (set in the same city and at approximately the same time) results from the way it creates the effect without total dependence on the accuracy of slang, costume and attitudes.

For persons who have worked on Guildless newspapers outside of the big chains, *Why Rock the Boat?* should be doubly effective in conjuring up this sense of what might be called *déja perdu*. It should be but it isn't, not completely. This is because Weintraub and the director John Howe base their satire on the technique of dividing up the characters into the straight ones and the caricatured ones. Among the underlings on the Montreal *Daily Witness* of the film, Gillard and Leek and Ken James (who plays Gillard's older pal, a randy photographer named Ronny Waldron) are fairly straight. Their truth rests in their typicality, in the fact that every newspaper seems to be full of individuals just like them. The same holds true for Sean Sullivan, who plays the browbeaten city editor, Herb Scannell. He's perfect and perfectly representative. All city editors have names like Herb Scannell. It's a requirement of the job. But the symbol of authority, the tyrannical managing editor Philip L. Butcher (played by Henry Beckman), is a grotesque exaggeration. He is every young reporter's nightmare of an M.E., a big square man who never speaks but bellows, whose cycle of hiring and firing is impossibly unpredictable and who smiles only once a year, when handing out the meagre bonuses at Christmas.

In this characterization and in a number of other ways, *Why Rock the Boat?* becomes another in the long series of newspaper comedies and melodramas that stretches back before the first filming of *The Front Page*, to *Five Star Final* in 1931 with Edgar G. Robinson, and probably beyond. It is a genre which reached its peak of triteness in the middle 1930s with all those zany comedies about the flippant reporter and the madcap heiress, usually played by someone resembling Carole Lombard. At its zenith, Warner Brothers made a number of them as a respite from their usual gangster films and they usually featured Frank McHugh as one of the funny-looking cynical reporters who never took off his hat.

Most of these films were written either by former newspapermen or by writers copying the writing of former newspapermen, and they came to have a great effect on the profession as well on civilians' ideas about the profession. This is a shame in a way since these movies have little to do with reality. The *Daily Witness*, for

16

example, seems to be staffed by only about twenty people, and though Howe used an old *Gazette* man named Jack Marsters as technical adviser, there are many little inaccuracies. Still, the film meets the demands of the Nostalgic Present because it's consistent with the public's idea of what newspaper people and newspapers are like. The newsroom is all frosted glass, wooden gates and crumpled paper on the floor, and folks still believe large dailies are like this. I know. I used to watch them taking tours of the Toronto *Star* and could see the disappointment in their eyes as they beheld the purple broadloom, the Scandinavian editing consoles and the expressionless faces of reporters in Jay Press suits.

Another but different catering to the public's persistent image of the press can be found in *I.F. Stone's Weekly*, a one-hour documentary on the maverick U.S. political commentator by Jerry Bruck, a Montreal filmmaker. This delightful film deals only on the surface with Stone's ideas and the importance of his articles in the late *Weekly* and more recently in *The New York Review of Books*. What it does instead is to bring alive one of the great myth figures of nineteenth-century America which Americans love to have resurrected for them. Izzy Stone is portrayed as that cousin and compatriot of the circuit rider and the frontiersman — the country editor.

We see the man who, when out of work during the McCarthy period, began his own little sheet but only after being turned down by seven printers. We see him reading voraciously, answering his own phone at a desk piled with clippings. We see him mailing his own newsletter at the box on the corner and crying a bit as he leaves the composing room after putting the last issue to bed. More importantly, we see his view of federal politics prevailing in the end. A sort of William Allen White of the Watergate era.

November – December 1974

II

The off-screen lives of movie stars, as much as their on-screen ones, have always been useful indicators of social change. Fatty Arbuckle's career was ruined by a sex scandal in 1921 while Errol Flynn's, a generation later, survived more than one rape trial. This points up a shift in the moral code and in society generally. Such people often do. In this context it's revealing to see Robert Redford lamenting for an interview in *Playboy* that "investigative reporting . . . seems to be a dying art in this country," and then concluding: "As a responsible, civil rights-minded citizen, I want to see more investigative reporting [because] this kind of reporting is a terrifically important part of our democratic process."

Redford was not merely speaking his mind, of course. He also was helping plug his planned film version of *All the President's Men*, the book by Bob Woodward and Carl Bernstein, the Washington *Post* reporters whose dogged leg work broke the Watergate cover-up story and won their paper a Pulitzer Prize. Redford purchased rights to the book for $450,000 and is to play Woodward to Dustin Hoffman's Bernstein. It's a case of recent events swaying a star's feelings and later his work, and of that work in turn helping to change the social structure further.

A mere two years ago Redford was playing a hip young Kennedyesque politician in *The Candidate*, a film that pretended to be cynical about the American political process. Now he's preparing to play the nemesis of the politician (and what's more, using his own money). The role he has chosen is not a new one in popular culture but it's one which, with the Year of Watergate over, is undergoing a spirited revival.

The signs of this revival are all around us. Two of last year's successful films dwell on the investigative reporter ferreting out truth. In *The Parallax View*, Warren Beatty is a newspaperman who witnesses a political assassination and is himself murdered when he gets too hot on the trail of the ring of killers. Later, in *The Odessa File*, John Voight is a young German magazine writer who tracks down a group of Third Reich veterans dedicated to the eventual rebirth of Nazism. In Voight's case, there is a personal motive: his father was killed during the war by the Nazi now being hunted. But the film's timeliness rests in more than the threat of rightwing takeover. It lies also in the pursuit of the Big Story by a dedicated newshound who cannot be bought and won't be intimidated.

18

The same trend is visible in recent movies closer to fact and also in books. *I.F. Stone's Weekly* by the Montreal filmmaker Jerry Bruck is not a movie about the Washington muckraker's ideas. It's not a film which presents various facts and then draws conclusions. What it does instead is to uncritically use Stone as a symbol for the reporter-as-hero, and this is what has made it popular, especially with the young.

All this activity stems, of course, from what the Americans term the Watergate crisis and everyone else calls the Watergate scandal, which also has had less visible, more important effects. Enrolment in schools of journalism in U.S. universities in 1973 jumped sixteen per cent and even larger gains are expected for 1974 and 1975. Even allowing for the usual percentage of these students who'll switch to dentistry or end up in public relations, this cannot be a bad thing journalistically as well as morally. Indeed, Richard Nixon, in making the underdog a fashionable necessity again, may be the best thing to happen to the newspaper business since the invention of the Linotype. What it's easy to forget amid all this is that popular interest in the muckraking journalist, as reflected in mass entertainment, is nothing new. It's been around a long time but until recently had been in disfavour, much as the press as a whole seemed to be until Watergate came along.

Until Redford announced his plans for the Woodward and Bernstein property it seemed that all the crusading reporter movies had already been made. It seemed in fact as though all the real newspaper films of the 1930s type, the kind in which the paper itself was as much a character as any of the actors, were finished for good. One of the last ones made in Hollywood was *–30–* , directed by and starring Jack Webb. But now even *The Front Page* has been remade, this time by Billy Wilder, with Jack Lemmon and Walter Matthau.

Like the potboiler novels about newspapers, these movies flourished until about the time of the Second World War. The novels, like Webb's film, were most often hypercharged dramas signifying nothing very much, while the films were usually romantic comedies. As the newspaper business battled first radio and hard times and then television, the films tended to become boardroom dramas rather than newsroom ones. Eventually the genre dried up almost completely and wasn't replaced to any great extent by movies dealing with television. Either television was too exotic or all too familiar a subject. Anyway, it lacked the necessary romantic tradition.

·19

While they lasted these movies spawned an interesting (and now, it seems, prophetic) subspecies: the movie of the inky crusader who had his cynicism penetrated by injustice and who went about righting other people's wrongs. The best of these perhaps was *Call Northside 777*, made in 1948, in which Jimmy Stewart's persistence and cleverness result in the freeing of Richard Conti, who's done eleven years in prison for a murder he didn't commit. More relevant to the current association of investigative reporting with political intrigue was the 1939 epic *Each Dawn I Die*. Here James Cagney is a reporter who's been sent up the river on a bum rap after refusing to water down his coverage of a political scandal. If this movie fades in the retrospective glow of the 1970s, it's only because even when playing the good guy Cagney never seems quite moral enough. Humphrey Bogart is much better, especially in *Deadline USA*, another film interesting in view of Watergate.

Here Bogey, the managing editor of a paper about to suspend publication, has uncovered the shady political connections of New York gangster Martin Gabel, who's otherwise remembered only as a panelist on *What's My Line*. Bogart decides to go out of business in a blaze of glory, ignoring threats of reprisal. The presses are ready to roll with the Big Story when Gabel (read John Mitchell) calls Bogart (Katherine Graham with a lisp), offering clemency one final time. Bogart refuses and makes an impassioned speech about the place of the press as public defender. At this signal, the conversation is drowned out by the din of the presses, printing the Truth. The film was released in 1952 and must certainly have begun to seem corny not long afterward. But it's surprisingly contemporary when seen today on the late show, though movies like this are being passed by in the rush to recapture the message they put across.

The trend will likely continue for a time, blending into the next one, whatever it will be, just as exorcism begat an earthquake. It will be interesting to see whether the TV networks — stung by the way they had the Watergate hearings handed to them after the newspapers had done all the work — will also take up the banner. A good guess is that they will — at least for as long as it's profitable to do so. One imagines at least one dramatic series about a big city reporter. He'll be the scourge of all those who say they aren't crooks when they are as well as of those who, like Jeb Stuart Magruder, enter into crime with foreboding, out of a sense of duty, but find their ethical compasses affected. There may well be such

20

a show next season. With good luck it will help people continue to be on guard. With bad luck it will star Sal Mineo and will be much too romantic. Inevitably, its effect will be to produce more PR men and dentists. It will be replaced, one can imagine, by a sitcom about a movie star whose political views immerse him in antics. The laughter will be canned. The dream will have been shelved, at least until the next big scandal excites the public mind.

Globe and Mail, January 4, 1975

III

The arts, you know — they're Jews, they're left wing — in other words, stay away.
> — Richard M. Nixon, tape of June 23, 1972

Alan Pakula's version of Carl Bernstein and Bob Woodward's book *All the President's Men* is a curious film that has already had a curious history and will leave behind it an equally curious legacy. One of the interesting aspects of it is that it operates on several levels of duality — as a total experience, as an end in itself, and as a bit of sociology. For example, the generality of laymen have been watching the film as both an anti-Nixon work and as a rendering into legend of something they themselves lived through and were part of. They have been entertained while at the same time they have been given proof of the stories they will tell their grandchildren. For people in the media, the dual expectations have been quite as distinct and even more contradictory.

21

People in the news racket are eager first of all to bask in the reflected glory of the Washington *Post*. At the same time they are anxious that the old hard-drinking flippancy of the Hollywood reporter be replaced by saner traits more in line with the dull reality of their lives. All that in turn is tied to and pitted against the basic set of contradictions inherent in the film itself. The amazing thing about *All the President's Men* is that it seems on the surface of it to satisfy everyone. It's a nice liberal film.

Pauline Kael, in her essay "Raising Kane," has already set in perspective the newspaper movie of the 1930s and how it came into being, reaching its finest artistic flowering the following decade in *Citizen Kane*. She better than anyone else to date has understood the effect of Ben Hecht and Charles MacArthur's play *The Front Page* on the newspaper business and the newspaper business' effect on the play. She stopped short of examining the larger question of the media's relation to their own idea of themselves. For that, one would have to go back to 1903 for films and for print at least back to Thackeray's *History of Pendennis* in 1848. But she did a good job of establishing the basic newspaper stereotypes so rampant in films. These stereotypes play an important part in *All the President's Men* in terms of both the story and the response to it of general and specialised audiences.

In the 1930s, newspaper people were almost as colourful as gangsters. Without the one the other couldn't have existed. The public knew that, like the gangsters, the newspapermen were crooked, but they enjoyed watching them being flamboyant about it. For the papers, it was good business to satisfy such expectations. Newspapers then had much less outside competition but were much more competitive with one another. The newspaper movie, made popular by Lewis Milestone's 1930 version of *The Front Page*, became a respectable genre. Warner Brothers (which also produced *All the President's Men*) excelled at grinding them out but was by no means the only studio to do so.

It was demanded of every leading man or incipient male star that he do time as a wisecracking reporter or tough-talking editor. The stereotypes grew from actual persons, often by way of precepts already established in cheap fiction. The result was that the stereotypes began to affect the reality. For generations newspaper people have gone out of their way to scorn the *Front Page* style; in recent years both *Time* and *MORE*, the left-wing journalism review, have mocked it in their house ads. But at the same time newsmen have

22

continued to incorporate the tradition into their lives as mistaken reality or as something somehow expected of them. What's seldom considered is the fact that the stereotypes have changed over the years, that there have been fashions in falsehood as in everything else. *All the President's Men*, far from being a new truth, is merely a revisionist distortion.

There were four principal stereotypes in the newspaper movies of old. First and foremost was the reporter. He was a fast-talking fellow who wore his hat in the office and called women sweetheart. He was always cynical, usually with good reason, but when it came to the big story he could be serious as well. The purest real life version of this type was probably Lionel Moise of Kansas City and Chicago. Every city, though, seems to have had ones like him. Each old reporter who wrote a novel or screenplay toyed with the *roman à clef* (Hildy Johnson of *The Front Page* was based on a man actually named Hildy Johnson). This character's cynicism peaked and ebbed according to the times. Gable in *Comrade X* and Jimmy Stewart in *Call Northside 777* were different sides of the same basic characterization.

Other stereotypes were the foreign correspondent and the girl reporter. The first was represented in real life by the likes of Richard Harding Davis and Vincent Sheehan and in film by, for instance, Joel McCrae in *Foreign Correspondent*. The second was, in actuality, Adela Rogers St. John and, in the myth, Bette Davis of *Front Page Woman* and Rosalind Russell of *His Girl Friday*. These two film glyphs, however, were always far less important than the last great stereotype, that of the editor. In films, the editor was a generic term meant to amalgamate Walter Howey, Stanley Walker, Henry Justin Smith, J. God Keely and, to hear newsmen tell it, just about every other famous editor who ever wielded a pencil stub. Like the reporter, the stereotypical editor changed according to the prevailing fashion without straying very far from his original usefulness.

The quintessential Hollywood editor of the 1930s was Lee Tracy. He wore tatty pinstripe suits and his brim turned up all the way around, and was the sadist in a sado-masochistic relationship with his staff. It was a role he walked through as late as 1943 in *The Power of the Press*. He was as unscrupulous as they come, and it was in some measure a new gimmick when, in *Five Star Final* of 1932, Edward G. Robinson played a Tracy-like tabloid editor who one day discovers principles (the role was probably inspired by Emile

23

Gravreau, a Canadian, who edited the incredible New York *Graphic*).

At any event, the distinguishing but never flatly stated fact about the Tracy-style editor was that he was a gentleman in an ungentlemanly business who behaved according to the latter circumstance rather than the former. He was rogue, but he was only a rogue among villains. In later versions of the stereotype this gentlemanliness was gone. Cagney in *Blood on the Sun*, Robert Ryan in *Lonelyhearts*, Bogart in *Deadline USA*, Gable in *Teacher's Pet* — all these were no-nonsense editors but none of them was at base a discredited gentleman. They were self-made men; they were graduates of the conservatoire of hard knocks rather than dropouts from Princeton, the way Tracy seemed to be, underneath. More so than Tracy, they were always gruffly nostalgic about the old days, when they could have got away with more garishness.

Throughout all such films (there must be hundreds of them) the dominant relationship, either on-camera or off-, was the cruelly symbiotic one of the older editor to the young reporter. This is where *All the President's Men* comes in. It is one of the greatest platonic love stories of the 1970s, a sort of Hecht and MacArthur Go To College.

It is fashionable to say of this film that here, at last, is a movie about real reporting rather than razzle-dazzle make-believe. Indeed it's true that the film is about reporting in the abstract, that it's about Nixon only if one chooses to make it so. Certainly it is only in this way that it will have any continuing interest, for five years from now no one will have heard of (for example) Maurice Stans, who figures prominently in the story.

The common view has been that the film is true-to-life because it shows what reporting is really about: hard slogging by telephone, endless fruitless interviewing and general leg-work, rather than the pyrotechnics of the 1920s and 1930s. So far so good. But that is also the film's limitation. *All the President's Men* is at base but a funny updating of the old editor-reporter love-hate two-step, which as much as anything else was always a story of the generation gap. Here, however, it is more complicated than previously.

Robert Redford as Woodward and Dustin Hoffman as Bernstein, though their characters are about the same age, represent in themselves one generation gap. Woodward is the type of clean-cut dullard who probably chose to study journalism because he flunked pre-med. He's a conservative in that he's a progressive,

24

concerned with the moment, to whom history is just a series of legal precedents. Bernstein, by contrast, is the typical kid who has worked his way up from copyboy without benefit of theory. He's a radical in that he's rooted in tradition and therefore knows what's been lost and what's at stake. He is the schizoid child of all the old movies which made him want to be a newsman in the first place. On the one hand, he's full of notions of responsibility and duty, like Bogart in *Deadline USA* but more frantic. On the other, he's like his journalistic forefathers in that he enjoys thinking of himself as a wordsmith when in truth he's only a typewriter jockey. Together he and Woodward are one conflict. They are pitted against another generation, embroiled in another conflict, in the form of Jason Robards as the Washington *Post* editor Ben Bradlee.

Robards, who looks, speaks and even moves here remarkably like the real Bradlee, is a throwback to Lee Tracy by being a soiled aristocrat. But he too is a victim of the movies in trying to disguise the fact by taking on the coarser toughness of a Cagney. The result is that, while he talks the profane newsroom patois amongst his underlings, to give them confidence in their communal enterprise, he behaves like a small man in a big world. He's afraid and respectful of his publisher. He lives in terror that his sources may not be informed. He encourages his charges to write like government auditors rather than scoundrels as though the government he's bringing down were composed of administrators, not criminals. *Gentlemen* [he seems to say condescendingly], *I address you privately. I want these people skewered but nothing too terribly Hollywood. I want it conducted on a high plane.* He sounds the way the late Vincent Massey would have sounded retaining the services of a hit man.

Based as it was exclusively on the work of Bernstein and Woodward, whose fault after all is that they're reporters who think and write like reporters, the film is, of necessity, distorted in its depiction of Watergate. Distorted not biased, though there is clearly an element of partisanship which makes the whole thing believable and enjoyable. It's distorted in that it leaves one with the impression that it was the Washington *Post* that brought down Nixon instead of the establishment.

Nixon was a Diefenbakerean sort of character. He repeatedly failed to ingratiate himself with the well bred rulers of society while claiming sympathy with the proles. Finally, the establishment did accept him because he seemed to be in keeping with the current whim of the fickle populace to whom lip service must be paid. Nixon, in his stupidity and vanity, thought he had actually been elected president instead of merely named front man. He acted accordingly and, in the end, was shot down for it. The *Post* was his Dalton Camp, a liaison between the front man and the chaps in the backroom. The New York *Times* (whose shop refused to set up ads calling for his impeachment) was the aristocratic patriarch, a cautious brahmin that could afford to appear liberal. It bided its time, however, until its uncle, the eccentric Chicago *Tribune*, called for Nixon's ouster. When *Time*, the epitome of new money, made the same demand, in the first editorial it had run since its founding in 1923, Nixon's fate was sealed. The chronology may be a bit off here but the thrust should be clear.

The point is not that Nixon was other than a rascal and turkey who deserved his fate. Far from it. He was and remains a despicable mammal who for thirty years tried establishing an alibi for his inadequacies by convincing himself that history admires and rewards neurotic war criminals. The point is merely that *All the President's Men* lends its full weight to the thesis that the *Post* singlehandedly did him in with the aid of perhaps a few Iscariots attempting to plea-bargain their way into heaven. This view of course is tommyrot, even poppycock. Nixon's option was dropped by those who had picked it up originally, by the conservatives who are so conservative that they still believe in the letter of the Constitution rather than the spirit of it.

Gone are the days when newspaper editorials can sway the opinions of the people on such important issues even if they were free to do so. Gone also are the days when the public at large mistakes attempted objectivity for plain neutrality. The point is that we should see this film for what it actually says about the press rather than what it appears or means to say. Beneath the veneer of authenticity — the exact-to-scale set of the *Post* newsroom, complete even to the television sets; and the cool and mannered professionalism of those who populate it — this is, like it or not, an old-fashioned scoop opera of the kind beloved by press club sclerosis sufferers. It has little to do with the truth because the facts are still at large. Instead it has to do with Walter Bradlee and Hildy Woodstein and the two possible page one proofs, one of which says FRAUD AT POLLS. On this Hollywood level it is quite well done, and downright engrossing. On the ideological, political and philosophical levels it's about as convincing as TV wrestling.

June – July 1976

26

IV

In the 1950s Paddy Chayefsky made television respectable. He was one of a group (others were Gore Vidal and Rod Serling) who brought drama to television and brought realism to television drama. But reputations made solely in TV, though they linger like the white dot in the centre of the screen, do not last. Chayefsky (who formerly spelled his name Cheyevsky) was remembered mainly for his teleplay *Marty*, which he later adapted for the screen — a medium to which it was not equal. Then, except for a few other screen credits, he disappeared. He disappeared so thoroughly that I can recall someone lamenting the loss of his "favourite writer, the lade Paddy Chayefsky." For a while he seemed a natural candidate for one of those Toronto *Star* whatever-became-of items, in which former Oscar winners and other titans are discovered, aged sixty-nine, living quietly in Scottsdale, Arizona, selling swimming pools.

Then, in 1971, Chayefsky returned to screenwriting. He received a second Oscar for *Hospital*, a blackly humorous look at the medical profession which brought together the seemingly disparate abilities of George C. Scott, Diana Rigg and Don Harron. *Hospital*, which did not do especially well critically or financially, was looked upon as improbable hokum by most everyone except doctors, nurses, interns and hospital administrators. *They* found it hilariously accurate — not too funny to be true but almost too true to be funny. Chayefsky's new screenplay *Network*, which is Oscar material if anything is, has much the same style and much the same effect on those in the know. *Network* is Chayefsky's revenge on television. It is the film equivalent of all those novels that old reporters threaten to write about their papers but seldom do, telling their colleagues that, what the hell, no one would believe it anyway.

The comparison with newspapers is not farfetched; in fact, I believe it central to an understanding of the impact of *Network*. The film could very well establish pervasive, almost unassailable stereotypes in the public's mind about the television industry. It could easily sink the business in a mire of myth and tradition that will be forevermore a source of warmth and rancour, doing for TV what the play *The Front Page* did for newspapers. Certainly the time is ripe for such an occurrence. The newspaper gargoyles that *The Front Page* and its imitators left in fiction, radio, television and, most importantly, movies, had begun to fade until Watergate.

Sometimes these stereotypes of newspaper people were updated as stereotypes of TV people. It is not entirely unreasonable, for example, that Clark Kent, in the comics, is no longer a reporter for the *Daily Planet* but a television news reader. Such transitions, however, were merely changes of costume; they were not original fashions tailored to the form of the electronic medium. For a long time it seemed that television by its very nature was incapable of creating a literature about itself. *Network*, I believe, shows that assumption to have been incorrect.

Like so much black humour, *Network* depicts not what will happen, nor even necessarily what could happen, but what one might very well perceive as happening. The film begins with a glimpse of an anchor on one of the American networks, played by Peter Finch (this bit of casting is about the only truly impossible bit: so British an anchorman on American television is unthinkable). Finch feels the world is too much with him and announces on-air that he will kill himself, also on-air, in one week's time. From the start his mental health is in question. But it is indicative of Chayefsky the black humorist, as distinct from the 1950s realist, that what once would have been the subject of a TV drama is now but a device for propelling, without explanation, a screenplay.

Finch, of course, is immediately blacked out and summarily fired from his job. The head of the news department, however, convinces management that his old friend should be allowed before the cameras a final time to offer a proper apology. This news executive, played by William Holden, is himself under assault from the network. Robert Duvall, installed by the conglomerate that has purchased the company, is casting a cold eye on the news operation's revenues. The head of entertainment programming, Faye Dunaway, is lusting after Holden's slice of the airtime and the budget. So, when Finch begins to apologize but ends sputtering obscenities and sounding like Charles Fort, Holden does not cut him off. He lets him ramble on as his own contribution to office politics. Here is black humour at its darkest: the sane but devious people taking advantage of the deranged but scrupulous one for the craziest of motives.

As it happens, Finch, in his rages, is actually in touch with the public, whereas the others are in touch only with ratings. Finch's tirade has drawn a huge audience, and he is given a new enlarged show of his own, complete with soothsayers and astrologers, to replace the network's nightly news. The programme is under the control of Dunaway. She has finally taken over the territory of Holden who, when sacked, promptly sets up housekeeping with her. Finch's popularity, of course, wanes in time. But he cannot be let go because the show is the favourite of the head of the conglomerate, who uses it as vehicle for Ayn Randish propaganda. There is no way for Dunaway to save her career but to have Finch assassinated. The man who was dismissed for threatening to kill himself is murdered on camera for not being so successful as he once was.

That's the plot, but the summary gives little indication of all the devious little turns, satires, one-liners and slaps in the face which Chayefsky has worked into *Network*, a film that is to him what *Modern Times* was to Chaplin. The script is more theatrical than anything else he has written in the curious sense of being more television-like. The pace is that of an upbeat magazine programme. Characters reappear to bridge neat little segments which, together, carry the story along episodically but frenetically. One is conscious throughout of watching a movie but in this case the realisation is part of the film's clever appeal. And it is a clever film, which is what many of the best U.S. films have always had to be before being great. Like *Citizen Kane*, *Network* uses slickness to awe one part of the audience and to add vicarious pleasure to the other part's awareness of what happens on a different level. The whole thing is so neatly blocked out, and then so carefully filled in, that there is little for the director Sidney Lumet to do but transfer the written word to the spoken word. They're a good team, Lumet and Chayefsky. Lumet's films are usually distinguished by great professionalism but lack any professional individualism. As for Chayefsky's contribution, *Network* is one of those uncommon films that proves the existence of the author as *metteur-en-scene* on at least equal footing with the director as *auteur*.

Network makes no bones, however, about being a film with as much polemical and sociological content as aesthetic content. The question then arises: What is it telling us about television? The answer, or answers, are frankly not very original or alarming. Chayefsky is saying, among other things, that TV news is merely showbiz, that TV careers are soul destroying, that TV executives have all the moral firmness of so many Saigon bambam girls with none of the redeeming earthiness. Surely no one has ever doubted these claims, just as no one with the remotest connection with the networks can deny having met real life equivalents of the Finch,

29

Holden, Dunaway and Duvall stereotypes. It is at this point that the *Front Page* comparison comes in.

To be sure, much of *Network* is at least inspired by truth. There was for instance actually a case — two years ago in Sarasota, Florida — of an anchor committing suicide live, so to speak. Certainly, the people now trying to identify the living counterparts of the stereotypes are not necessarily foolish to do so. Fifty years back it was fashionable to play the same game with the characters in the Hecht-MacArthur play. Assuming that *Network* will carve its stereotypes in stone, as I think it could do in time, the real question should be: why are the two pieces of writing so effective in the same way?

Neither is the first of its kind, although they may both come to be remembered that way. There were plays and even movies about the newspaper racket before *The Front Page*, even some that sought to portray its venal side. But they were mainly intended to inform and to shock. They tried to create a furor about the American scandal press as it then existed. Hecht and MacArthur had no such intentions. They were veterans of yellow journalism looking back with loving nostalgia to what the public was already resigned to accepting as truth. The play had such great impact because its literary excellence (the dialogue stands up beautifully) reassured the patrons that reality could not hurt them once stereotypes were made from bogeymen. The play dealt of course with corruption and the low sort of journalism (the *Herald-Examiner* was after all a Hearst paper) but it was a humanistic piece of work. It showed that rough edges could be used as art.

So it is with *Network*. There have been other works on the same theme. Within the past five years, for instance, a shelf of novels about television have appeared — Ned Calmer's *The Anchorman*, Al Morgan's *Anchorwoman*, Jim Lowe's *Network* (no relation), Noel B. Gerson's *Talk Show*, Jack Ansell's *Dynasty of Air*, Dan Jenkins and Edwin Shrake's *Limo*. There are probably others. Each was a *roman à clef* seeking to be an exposé as well. They take the same attitude towards television as Chayefsky's script, one no different after all from that presented in the book and film of Jacqueline Susann's *Love Machine*.

It is only now, however, that anyone has made a serious work of art using TV as the subject. Only now have we become completely blasé about television's effects. The mass insouciance has taken the place of the calm and distance that artists usually need to gain

30

perspective. The process is part of the curious American system of incorporating horror stories into popular mythology and the mythos into popular culture. *Network* is a sort of *Citizen Kane* with a notion for a subject, a *Front Page* without the surprises. Watching it, one knows what is coming, and laughs wryly. The script ticks off the seconds leading — not to the destruction of our cherished prejudices — but confirmation of our folly in believing them. Watching it gives some idea of how it must have been seeing Shaw for the first time in the 1890s or stumbling upon the unknown Mencken a decade later. The film debunks what we're already tired of reviling. It does so with some brilliance.

February 1977

The Anti-Social League

I

Paul Schrader, author of the screen-plays for such features as *Obsession*, *Rolling Thunder*, *The Yakuza* and *Taxi Driver*, ran into problems during the pre-production stages of *Blue Collar*, his first film as a director. The script he wrote with his brother Leonard Schrader concerns the working and emotional lives of three labourers on a car assembly line. But none of the big four auto makers in Detroit would let him use their plants for location shooting. He did finally manage, however, to get permission from the Checker Motor Company in faraway Kalamazoo, a firm which, because its business is making taxis, is apparent-ly less concerned with its consumer image. The conclusion to be drawn from this is not necessarily that taxis are a continuing symbol in Schrader's work. It is interesting to note, however, that Checker (which he places in Detroit anyway) is known throughout the film by its real name, while the United Auto Workers is transmogrified into the Amalgamated Automotive Workers.

Blue Collar is a movie that's pretty realistic in presenting the viewpoint of the underclass. For its three characters, the union comes to seem even more exploitative than the company. The three characters are Richard Pryor, Harvey Keitel and Yaphet Kotto. They're poor bastards struggling without much success simply to stay where they are in the world. The problem is not that they lack control over their environment and feel what they do is unrewarding. Nor are they Upton Sinclair characters whose consciousnesses need raising by some avenging Walter Reuther. It's a case, rather, of their being confined by the tripartism of employer, union and family to the point where they feel justifiably claustrophobic and worthless. (Another director would have made a film about the *families* of such people — but most would have settled for worse than *Blue Collar*, a film like *The Betsy*, which goes on for two hours, covers fifty years of Detroit automotive history and doesn't show us so much as a black extra.) Anyway, the principals of *Blue Collar* are not ambitious and maybe have given up even aspiring to be. They're ordinary guys to the point of being self-destructive. Such roles are so difficult to handle convincingly that most actors either fall back on accents and dialect to do the work or else make the characters different sorts of people entirely who happen to be down on their luck. To their considerable credit, Schrader and his cast attempt far more than this, though with wildly uneven results.

Blue Collar starts out soberly enough, with each character establishing himself at length. Kotto plays an ex-con, a huge hulk of a man who knows his own strength perfectly well, though prison has left him cautious and seemingly at peace. His performance has just the right touch of ghetto eloquence. Keitel's character, whom local parlance would have it is a dumb Pollack, is a more troubled soul. The system has not yet beaten him into serenity, and he's frustrated at finding that natural intelligence is in itself no solution to his problems. Pryor, for his part, has more difficulty than the other two actors. He never seems quite sure if the lines Schrader has written for him are outside the character's vocabulary. The result is that he breaks into comedic delivery much of the time as though playing a guy playing Richard Pryor. When he does so during serious scenes he's offputting. The habit is less annoying when it comes during Schrader's long burst of silliness in the middle of the film.

33

What we see in the first half is background. The action doesn't begin until, one night in a bar, the three auto workers decide to solve their money problems by burgling the offices of their union local (what the hell's the union ever done for us anyway? they ask). Here, for no very good reason, they suddenly become Larry, Moe and Shemp and the prevailing tone one of slapstick. They find no cash but only a ledger. This, they learn later, records the misuse of union funds for loanshark operations, apparently in partnership with the Mob. But by then the film has sharply changed course once again and become a veritable tag-team match of wrestling-with-one's-conscience and losing.

Slowly the three convince one another to blackmail the union, which in turn takes its insurance company for a bundle on the robbery claim. But when they've made themselves known as the ones with the account book, they're first threatened and then attacked. In a particularly grim scene, Kotto is murdered by being locked in a windowless room with automatic paint-sprayers, where he's asphyxiated. Then the union bosses try winning over Pryor and Keitel with a little blackmail of their own. At first both resist. Their privileged look at how the union and the industry are actually run lets them see that the one side is just as bad as the other, that it's only by continuing the tension between white and black, rich and poor and management and labour that the bosses on both sides prosper. Pryor, though, gives in. He becomes a shop steward, exchanging his blue collar for a white one and for some of the spoils. He tells Keitel (but really himself) that he's taking the job so as to change the system from the inside. But his rationalising degenerates into an embarrassed whisper.

Keitel is the last one dealt with. Attempts are made on his wife and children. Then he's followed in his car by henchmen with a shotgun. He thinks of going into exile when he sees a sign indicating the tunnel to Canada (not an easy feat from Kalamazoo, by the way, which is about two hundred miles from the border). Finally he too accepts a union post but also gets trapped into becoming an FBI stoolie. So at the end of the film we've got Pryor working for a union that's in league with the underworld and Keitel betraying these infidels by secretly working for a government that regards such unholy alliances as unfair competition. The wonder, when you think about it, is not that the union needed a fictional name but whether the whole society should sue for libel, were it not for the fact truth is often a defence under law.

There's a sense in which *Blue Collar* is a step forward for Schrader as an artist generally and at least a subtle half-step for him as a screenwriter. His early films seem now to concern the idea of the subculture, not really any one subculture in particular. But they felt bound to present themselves as being psychologically earnest and sociologically relevant — and only then as humanly interesting, with the infusion of a little compassion. *Taxi Driver*, I believe, changed all that by reversing the order. His script worked well with Martin Scorsese's pyrotechnic direction but also laid a foundation of humaneness beneath it. The simple visual story of a single personality was there for those who wanted it. Likewise the cinematic razzmatazz. But there was also that special element of artistry that elevated the project and made it more complex than either the story or the flashy direction could have done, singly or together. Schrader was finally forcing himself to think in pictures *in order* to bring out his character's instincts, instead of devising images and then making them fit psychologically.

By contrast, *Blue Collar* is a simpler, more obvious film of no special grace technically. But it does show that Schrader is continuing to explore the underclass who have no access to the attention of others — exploring it without lapsing into some Dylanesque mythology of the disenfranchised and without disguising his work as sociological voyeurism. The film may look and read at times like an old Haldeman-Julius pamphlet and at others like a slickly plotted TV show that can't make up its mind. But it's about real people who don't have credit cards, never get their names in the papers and were moved by the death of Elvis in ways they never could have been touched by the concurrent demise of Groucho. If Schrader can bring his directing and basic filmmaking abreast of his screenwriting he's going to be subversive in the best sense of the word.

May 1978

35

Fashions within movies have always changed a great deal faster than the fashions for movies. Even so, while musicals, westerns and other genre films still get made, they are less dependable moneymakers than they once were, especially if they are big budget productions. The slide into unpredictability had more to do with television than with the decline of the major studios, though the two factors are interdependent. The 1960s put fresh life into some odd types — spy films, for instance — but the film-makers made too many of them, television even more, and soon we all wearied of the exercise. There is, however, one kind of film that has flowered fully in the past decade. We have not yet tired of it mainly because we have yet to understand it.

For want of a better term such films can be called urban picaresques. They are never popular enough to be a fad or a fashion. Neither are they genre pictures, since what they have in common is more a sensibility than a formula. Historically their roots go back to Preston Sturges' *Sullivan's Travels* and Mervyn LeRoy's *I Am a Fugitive from a Chain Gang*, although they lack the 1930s altruism of those examples. The films I have in mind are difficult to label except by example or by comparison with what they are not. Minor as most of them are commercially, the have had their imitators, and that fact makes classification even more difficult.

A certain view of the class structure is one attitude such films share. They are picaresques in that they're about persons who are outcasts — deliberately outcasts, though sometimes uncomprehendingly and even inevitably so. The films strive to give the audience an idea of how the other class lives. They're set not so much in the underworld as on the fringes of dominant structure, which is to say beyond the common notion of respectability. The people in them live outside the huge middle section of society upon which neither wealth nor poverty makes much impact. They're not part of the alternate culture for "alternate" suggests disavowal. Instead, they are about the *other* culture, whose greatest weapon but also greatest threat from the outside is everyone else's myopia. That myopia is perhaps the reason most such films are not very financially successful. They ridicule, often without humour and usually without much effect, the people who constitute the customary cinema audience. People respond to most films by thinking: "What I've seen is a possible reality but the movies about it are just movies." After picaresques they say to themselves: "Reality like that exists *only* in the movies."

Thus *The Graduate* was not a picaresque because it was about someone who was merely alienated from the main culture, who belonged to it however much it frustrated him. Haskel Wexler's *Medium Cool*, by contrast, *was* a picaresque because it concerned someone with little place in the main culture who paid the penalty for being so.

Such films depend for their sensibility on the director's detachment from the world of the audience. Respectability is something one either has or hasn't. It takes a skilled and talented respected person who is at least some sort of outsider to attempt such movies. John Schlesinger, for example, as an Englishman and a theatre type, was enough of an outsider to imagine himself even more of one. The result was *Midnight Cowboy*, which seems a picaresque because of its detachment, though in truth the film was laundered. It had too high a ratio of atmosphere to substance, too much reporting and too little raw sensation. Ratso, to Schlesinger, was more a character, in the colloquial sense, than an individual. Possibly that's one reason the film was so successful at the box office.

There's always someone more outcast than oneself just as there's always someone hipper, and a number of people have better outsider vision than Schlesinger. One of them is Bob Rafelson. His three films — *Five Easy Pieces, The King of Marvin Gardens,* and *Stay Hungry* — are fine examples of the picaresque. Significantly, the first was the least picaresque and the most commercial. The other two, true to the attitudes behind them, seem likely to have long lives in repertory and university rentals, those being the principal markets for picaresque films. There is a great paradox here: television almost destroyed the feature film industry but also tore down the barriers to picaresques by capturing the market for old values. Such films are allowed to exist by their very failure to convert an audience that has moved on and backwards.

There seem to be three approaches to dealing with the attitudes necessary to picaresque films. One is straight drama, as in *Panic in Needle Park, Mickey One* or *Fat City.* Films of that type often provoke only limited mass response. They fail to convince the audience that the reality depicted, though different from their own, is equally valid. Partly the failure is due to certain problems of technique: because they are modal rather than substantial, picaresques are weak on plot and predictability and tend to reach peaks of atmosphere rather than action. Mainly, though, they fail to convince because the world they depict is picaresque not picturesque, and the audience cannot grasp the difference or doesn't want to grasp it.

The second avenue is comedic. In taking this approach, the filmmaker will try converting audiences to his different reality by ridiculing their own through caricature. Thus *Bye Bye Braverman* made fun of *Commentary* intellectuals, *Move* of dominant culture lowbrows and *The Ruling Class* of a British upper crust really meant to represent the audience. The difficulty comes, and it usually does, when people laugh for the wrong reasons, when viewers think the joke is on their neighbours not themselves. A fine instance is the scene in *Greetings* in which an assassination conspiracy buff becomes so caught up in his theories that he begins tracing bullet trajectories on the body of the person he's in bed with. The audience laughed — but only at conspiracy buffs.

A third approach to the picaresque (which often overlaps the other two) is to introduce a straight character into the picaresque world. In that way the director hopes for audience identification with the character symbolising them. He wishes them to share his sensations as they do those of the stranded traveller calling for assistance at the castle that is, unbeknownst to him, haunted. Two such films are *T.R. Baskin* and (sort of) *Easy Rider*. Another (also sort of) is *Electra Glide in Blue*. Such films don't work as they should because the picaresque characters are mistaken for mere anti-heroes; that is, dominant culture types who are psychologically or socially flawed. Such films are even worse failures socially when the picaresque characters are represented by symbols, thus throwing everyone into confusion. An example is *The Last Run*, with George C. Scott, in which an entire genre of film (namely, Bogartian sentimental tough guy pictures) symbolised but failed to penetrate the social reality beneath.

The present danger is that urban picaresques may become a genre in themselves, fossilised as failures instead of successes. The process is already underway. Martin Scorsese, for example, has been truly a director of picaresques. But he is a filmmaker first and an outsider second, and seems continually to wink at the audience. He is similar in that way to Brian DePalma whose new film *Obsession*, even more than his earlier one *Sisters*, owes greater allegiance to Hitchcock than to its own attitudes. There is the danger that both directors will become Bogdanovichs, making sequels to films that never really existed; that they will become to film what Tom Waits is to blues: imitators fanning out to catch more nuances instead of closing in to make stronger and stronger statements.

December 1976 – January 1977

Scorsese, Ashby &
Mazursky

I

In a novel there is at least an apparent atten-
tion to considerations of probability: it is a
narrative of what might occur. Romance flies
with a free wing and owes no allegiance to
likelihood. Both are fiction, both works of the
imagination, but should not be confounded.
They are as distinct as beast and bird.
— Ambrose Bierce

It seems certain that the type of person who devoured the works of mid-
dlebrow fiction writers in the 1920s —
devoured not Dreiser and Dos Passos
but Elinor Glyn, Michael Arlen or
even James Branch Cabell — today
devour instead the works of middle-
brow directors. This is probably all to
the good of both literature and film,
and anyway it is hardly a new realisation. What's interesting is the fact that
for some time movies have been
made which are predicated on this
mellifluous shift in public taste.

In the 1920s and for some indeter-
minate time afterwards there still existed whole blocs of people who were

romantics — who believed that life would turn out as it did in romances, as Bierce (who seemed to be paraphrasing Hawthorne's introduction to *The House of the Seven Gables*) defined them. They thought that good would triumph over probability so long as one plodded along a chapter at a time, acting out one's prosy imitation of life.

Few such people exist today. Now what we have instead are cinematics, people who believe that life will turn out the way it does in Hollywood films. These are people (and who among us isn't one?) whose surroundings are visual rather than descriptive and who fully believe that, while they may be only anti-heroes, at least they will meet an anti-hero's end; that life, however grotty it becomes, will still be picaresque and therefore interesting; and that no matter how good or bad things seem, they can always start afresh when the lights come up again.

It would be difficult to determine exactly when the cinematics came to prominence, but it's not hard at all to list recent films dealing with dreamers of this type. Peter Pearson's *Paperback Hero*, for instance, was, contrary to its title, about a cinematic rather than a romantic, and then there are more obvious examples such as *Gumshoe* and *The Projectionist*. One could go on and on. Perhaps the most cohesive of these films so far is *Alice Doesn't Live Here Anymore*, the new work by Martin Scorsese, who made *Mean Streets*.

Cinematics' films are a subspecies of nostalgia films, the roots of which in present society already have been examined to death. Scorsese classifies cinematics' movies still further. His films treat cinematics as an ethnic group and use another ethnic group to drive home the point. The autobiographical *Mean Streets*, which he also wrote, concerned young New York Italians who had grown up believing they had to be tough guys, long after the practical need for being tough guys had passed. They felt this way partly because they had been reared on tough guy movies, which had taken the place of familial instruction. *Alice Doesn't Live Here Anymore* employs a similar concept but with two differences of fact. The first is that the dream of happiness in show business (rather than mere success in show business) has replaced here the tough guy dream. The second is that Alice is not of course an Italian but a member of that oppressed majority, womankind.

Alice, superbly realized by Ellen Burstyn, the mother in *The Exorcist*, is shown in a childhood flashback committed to the idea of becoming a fluorescent torch singer, like Alice Faye in the 1940s

41

movies so important in her youth. Before her marriage and removal to Socorro, New Mexico, she even had a try at professional singing, in Monterey, California. In her imagination, Monterey has remained the capital of an amorphous Hollywood: a place where reality is made to order and all things can come to pass. The script, by Robert Getchell, concerns her circuitous pilgrimage to Monterey, freedom and stardom following the death of her husband in his Coca-Cola truck. It is a predictable film in many ways, a female road picture not without clichés; but it works because it is so well written, acted and directed.

The other central fact about Alice, after the fact of her cinematicism, is that she has bad luck with men, or rather with males. Her husband was a brutish jock gone to seed and turned sullen. Her eleven-year-old son (played by Alfred Lutter), who accompanies her on this hegira, is one of those kids with an adult's profane vocabulary and a level of destructive energy remarkable at any age. His relationship to her is like a dog's to its master. To him, his mother's bursts of rage and affection are mysterious and unpredictable; he looks up with his big floppy ears never knowing if he's going to be petted or hit with a rolled-up newspaper. Hers to him is the same relationship reversed. She finds this frightening and tries to keep from thinking about the fact that this boy will someday grow into some sort of man, perhaps a variety of cowboy. Cowboys are her bane. Her husband was one of sorts, and soon she finds another.

As mother and child make their way from New Mexico to northern California they are constantly immersed in what used to be called antics. At one of the first stops, Alice manages to get work in a piano bar, the low quality of which matches the quality of her singing voice. While there she meets a slickered-up urban cowboy with a string tie and a line of fast talk. She runs out on this relationship when his wife appears from the woodwork. The lover bursts in on the two women talking together and smashes up Alice's motel apartment. Alice and the boy hastily move to the next town, where she is reduced to waiting table in a diner. It's an uproarious place, and it is here that the comic height is reached in what is anyway a funny film. In several scenes one expects to see a barrage of cream pies thrown not in impishness but exasperation.

Much has been made of *Alice Doesn't Live Here Anymore* as a film of the women's movement, and there is more than a little truth in this view. Alice is a thoroughly contemporary if hapless sort of heroine, whose desire for a career has lain a long time just beneath the surface, to rise only after her husband's physical — but also symbolic — death. But if all the males in the film (except possibly her son) are mere caricatures of maleness, this is for other than ideological reasons. It's because Alice (named perhaps for Alice Faye herself) is such a cinematic that her vision is always clouded. And this film is shot through Alice's eyes as much as through a camera lens.

The last man Alice meets along the road is played by Kris Kristofferson and he too is a caricature, one every bit as familiar as the others but more likeable by being less bitterly drawn. He's the young divorced rancher she encounters in the hash-house. They spend time together on his nearby spread, and it's all quite idyllic until he loses his temper at the eleven-year-old's rascality. This throws Alice into a welter of atavistic motherly emotions, and the lovers themselves set to arguing. She is tempted to make up with him but also tempted not to. The decision is whether to take a gamble on happiness on the ranch or pursue further the elusive career in Monterey. The latter is a thought now less appealing than before in view of the brushes with real life the journey has afforded. In the end, we are left to suppose that Alice chooses the first course. But we're not certain. Scorsese leaves us dangling and thus shows that *Alice Doesn't Live Here Anymore* is almost as autobiographical as *Mean Streets*, though more subtly so. Scorsese in fact *is* Alice. He, like her, has grown up in a perpetual movie that affected all five senses and, again like his character, doesn't know whether he's quite ready for reality even now. Scorsese himself is the biggest cinematic of all and that's why the film works as well as it does, which is rather well indeed.

April – May 1975

◆

Martin Scorsese's *Taxi Driver* establishes him as the peer of Francis Ford Coppola and thus one of the two most significant U.S. film-makers of his generation. It also makes the star, Robert De Niro, one of the most impressive actors since Brando in his prime. These statements may startle but they should not surprise. *Taxi Driver* merely fulfils the promise that was obvious in both men's earlier

43

and less ambitious films. The two work in tandem in a way director and actor seldom do. They produce a film that, for all its many flaws, is far ahead of other contemporary movies in power and immediacy. By comparison, *Dog Day Afternoon* was a television programme and *Nashville* a comic strip with pretensions, which the latter may have been anyway. Scorsese and De Niro are children of the times. In concert they have made a film that is incredibly true not to the actualities of the day (perhaps that's one of the flaws) but to the present mood. It's not a static document. It's a movie. It *moves*. Its power and importance lay in the way the film and the audience work together, the one stirring up the other's emotions, which are then put back into the watching. Perhaps this contributes to the fact that *Taxi Driver* is an on-the-one-hand, on-the-other-hand type of experience. It's in those terms anyway that it has to be reviewed.

What has been obvious about Scorsese was that he has unusual street savvy. He does not come from the middle class and he has mixed feelings about the fact. On the one hand, he tries establishing his identity apart from the horde by showing that his background and attitudes are different from theirs and something to be proud of. On the other hand, he resents the majority, who look upon such people as cute aberrations, and so there is bitterness in his voice. What in *Boxcar Bertha, Mean Streets* and even *Alice Doesn't Live Here Anymore* was this duality of attitude is, in *Taxi Driver*, a single sensibility. The character De Niro plays, a New York cabbie, is the dispassionate embodiment of Scorsese's contradictions. Scorsese can get away with it because he's the kind of independent director who couldn't have existed a few years ago. He does what he damn well pleases. He has ancestors without having a tradition. The result is that *Taxi Driver* has neither Hollywood slickness nor the anti-slickness that comes through deliberate disavowal of Hollywood.

It is a tendency of American films (and of first novels everywhere) that they fall apart at the end. The present film does so too but the blame must be shared by the writer Paul Schrader, a hitherto unknown whose script deserves, and receives, billing equal to Scorsese's. The fault, if fault it is, is in no way traceable to De Niro. In *Mean Streets* and later *The Godfather II* he overcame the memory of his first film *Greetings* and showed himself an actor of quiet intensity and understated power who by his very silence and understatement made you keep watching, waiting for the explosion that

44

never came. He was a sort of Rod Steiger but with subtlety, imagination, and without formula pretense, who wanted only a chance to do his stuff. In *Taxi Driver* he keeps pulling out the stops right to the end, even after the direction and the script have broken down.

Travis, the character played by De Niro, is a young Marine veteran. This alone is enough to assure him a place on the fringes of commerce. He's one of those poor schmucks home from Nam with little but the ability to take apart an M-16 blindfolded and put it back together: a not very marketable skill even in New York City. He acts stupid with the boss when we first see him, applying for a hack-driving job. He acts this way (we later learn) not because he is in fact dumb but because he's learned that playing dumb is the best way to survive his superiors. And just everybody is his superior.

It is this peerlessness that is perhaps his problem. He drives madly around New York trying to make money, even going to Harlem at night (one of the incredible bits, this. There's no mention of gipsy cabs and De Niro is a bit too slight of frame to take on 110th Street). He is attracted by the stability of the class above him, personified here by Cybill Shepherd, a campaign worker for a rising young U.S. senator. But he's also repulsed and angered by the way such people corrupt and cinematise his kind of experience. When he confronts lowlife in the streets, however, his feelings are just as mixed. He aspires to the attitude of his betters and thinks the people he lives among are scum — not only that but scum unknowingly competing with him for the honours of degradation. Yet he is really no better than the scum and he knows it. Remembering his own tackiness, he feels sympathetic and finally protective towards them. This side of his life and consciousness is expressed by twelve-year-old Jodie Foster. She does a fine job of portraying a twelve-year-old hooker who's too experienced for her own good.

At the centre of the film is the fact that Travis is a dangerous psychotic. He is in actuality the lone madman the Warren Commission took Lee Harvey Oswald to be. He buys handguns on the black market and begins prowling the streets with the meter off looking for someone to shoot. By shooting someone even lower on the ladder than himself he may attain — what? — fame and glory, or the feeling that he's joined the tidy dominant society, or that he's reclaimed his own inheritance of violence? It is one of the great strengths of *Taxi Driver* that Scorsese doesn't try for phoney psychology. The truth is that human psychology has divorced itself from veterinary medicine but has failed to do its job; that there is in fact no explanation for such behaviour, only intellectual exercises as postmortems. Travis is not crazy because he thinks he is or because he believes he's sane and we disagree. He's crazy simply because he's outside the realm of our experience and we can't understand him. He's merely in touch with a reality different from ours. Scorsese is wise in believing that reality is in the eyes of the beholder, not something established by show of hands.

Another director would have handled the question of derangement differently and worse. He might have done away with the imponderableness of it all (and much of the film's power) by showing Travis to be suffering from something tangible, such as a brain tumour. Or he might have shown him to have been injured psychologically in the war. Someone else might well have resorted to flashbacks of the jungle. Scorsese makes the war an integral part of Travis without even alluding to it. The whole question is brought into play subtly. In fact there is no mention of Vietnam at all.

With the kind of logic brought only by madness (it resembles the careful diction aroused by drunkenness) Travis decides he must get back into shape if he's going to succeed in his mission. He decides he must regain the sense of belonging that the Marine Corps, all else you can say about it, instills in people. We see him shining his shoes in the military manner: dipping the cloth first in water and then in two tins of paste he's first passed over with a match. We also see him doing military style push-ups. It is in an aerial shot of this act, lasting only a few seconds, that we catch a glimpse of a terrible bloody scar on his back which we know could have been incurred only in the war. That is the only real statement of his service. It's also a possible explanation for his actions for those who choose the security of such an easy answer.

Taxi Driver is full of wonderful scenes and some dire nonsense. De Niro considers assassinating the clean-cut but conniving politician (a stereotype or a representative?) but is foiled in the plot. What finally happens is that he bursts into the teenaged whore's Lower East Side tenement, first having killed her streetcorner pimp and the building superintendent. Inside the apartment, he kills one of the girl's customers and is himself severely wounded — too severely for him to be up and around as quickly as he seems to be later. This is where the film falls apart.

46

Scorsese has made the extended shooting spree, the climax of an otherwise gut-honest film, a ballet. His violence and bloodbath are the choreographed kind associated with such diverse films as *Bonnie and Clyde*, *A Clockwork Orange* and virtually the entire corpus of Sam Peckinpah. This is a shame, for it was one of the strengths of *Mean Streets* that Scorsese seemed to know that violence doesn't rehearse, that it just happens, then just as quickly goes away, like the wicked messenger in the Dylan song. Another failure is the coyness and fake Hollywood irony of the plot from that point on.

De Niro recovers from his wound to find himself a media hero. It seems the fellow he killed in the bedroom was a big mafioso. Scorsese pans across Travis's wall to show pasted-up newspaper clippings attesting to both facts. The clippings, however, are clearly some set-director's mock-ups. Besides, such a story just would not be played as these clips have treated it. One big headline in the *Daily News* and that would be it. A little 96-pt. Marathon condensed and it would be all over. Just why a mob guy would be in the company of a child prostitute in such a place, instead of in some restaurant with a seeing-eye blonde, is not explained. The simple triumph of kinkiness over caution is not a satisfactory answer. The ending is annoying not only in these inconsistencies but in its uncharacteristic reversion to the Hollywood of old, where law decreed that loose ends had to be tied up, however ludicrously. No doubt the ending is a small concession to the audience, who in all other matters of interpretation are given a great deal of leeway, perhaps more than many of them prefer.

Is the film about the rot that's setting into New York and perforce the whole society? Well, most people know very little about cities in the nineteenth century and almost nothing about current society. Is it about the dangers of lunatics cut off from the rest of us who burst into our lives, literally, with a vengeance? Or is it a psychological study without more general social implications? There are also particular aesthetic conundrums, such as the musical score by the late Bernard Herrmann, who wrote the music for, among other films, *Citizen Kane*. Was he so behind the times that he composed a 1940s score for a 1970s film? Or did he purposefully use jazz and heavy strings to increase the uncertainty and the drama? The film can be taken as a terrifying mess of undeniable power or, on another level, as an overwhelming novelistic film using every trick, gimmick and technique Scorsese has been able to inherit, copy or manufacture. The truth probably lies some-where in between: *Taxi Driver* is the flawed masterwork of a new order that, by its unintentional imperfections, jars us awake from time to time, making our participation much more valuable and the total experience all the more rewarding.

May 1976

No one got off to a better start than Martin Scorsese and no other has got so carried away with splinter enthusiasms. His fondness for streetwise, parlourdumb characters has now led him to the old-time jazz ethos, the world in which people keep repeating that they have to get out of the cellars, man, and drink themselves to sleep over some early failure to retain their mechanical rights. His latest film, *New York New York*, is about one such person (Robert De Niro) and his relationship with a singer (Liza Minnelli). A musical set in the 1940s, it offends at first viewing only because, unlike all other musicals, it is not happy. Careful consideration, however, reveals the other reasons. These are that the film is too long, the script too slack, and Minnelli too cute. De Niro, poor man, gets no help from anyone else on either side of the camera. It becomes a one-man show by default as he tries to do his best to salvage the film. Nice period touches, though. Scorsese and Minnelli are now doing a stage musical together.

December 1977 – January 1978

Martin Scorsese was there in San Francisco filming the whole affair when, two years ago, the Band gave the farewell concert its mem-bers called the Last Waltz. But judging by his film record (also entitled *The Last Waltz*), Scorsese was not giving the matter his full attention. As a documentary the film is cloying because it shows no deliberate understanding of what the Band was and whence it came. Also, Scorsese practically ignores the extent to which the evening for those present was an event and not just a performance;

he shows almost nothing of the five thousand people who were fed sumptuously, who danced and otherwise participated in that massive feast of thanksgiving. He concentrates almost exclusively on the series of performances. But he breaks the rhythm of these by intercutting interviews he personally conducted with Robbie Robertson, Rick Danko, Richard Manuel, Garth Hudson and Levon Helm. And as an interviewer, Scorsese is fetchingly incompetent, with the fumbling uninformed style of someone you'd expect to find on educational television very early in the morning or very late at night. Yet *The Last Waltz* does have its special strength, in the person of Robbie Robertson, even though this strength was, by its forcefulness, the fatal weakness of the group.

Robertson was the Band's principal writer and leading natural resource. It was he who led the transition from their being Ronnie Hawkins' backup and then a Yonge Street bar band to being Dylan's colleagues and an entity in their own right. In the early days, Levon Helm, the only non-Canadian of the five, had been the nominal leader, but this didn't fool anyone who saw or heard the Band in its later incarnations. Throughout the film (which, naturally, he produced as well) Robertson is absolutely unaffected and ingratiating as he tries to compensate for the dullness of Scorsese and the somewhat strained gaiety of his fellow musicians. His presence is totally winning, and he'd be wise to include acting among the careers he and the others are now pursuing independently of one another.

It's plain from the film that, without trying to dominate, Robertson far outstripped the others in the field of applied talent and that this factor, not the fatigue they all profess on camera, was what caused them to disband — er, so to speak. While more pleasant and fascinating to watch than those in *Let It Be*, the vibes and intimations of group mortality in *The Last Waltz* are no more subtle. Just as intriguing are Robertson's animated remarks about his musical influences. His most respected songs so far have been the historical ones. But it's clear that these spring not so much from an acute historical sense (compared with Randy Newman's or Dylan's) as from a love of the history of popular music itself. This attraction, of course, was the dominant element of the Band's music between and after their successive breaks from Hawkins and Dylan. Perforce it was also the grounds, indirectly, for annulment.

October – November 1978

49

II

Hal Ashby's *Shampoo* didn't seem a better movie in anticipation than it did in retrospect but it certainly seemed as though it was going to be much different than it is. Advance publicity in the trade press and elsewhere stated that Julie Christie would be teamed once more with the film's producer Warren Beatty, a much underappraised actor who has been compensating for this by working hard and choosing carefully. It also informed us that Beatty had written the script with Robert Towne, possibly the most interesting new screenwriter afoot. What's more, by way of icing the cake, we were told that Paul Simon would be composing and performing the score. This was to be a serious film, set in California in the 1960s, about the relationship between political immorality and private promiscuity. It is in fact an enjoyable film, not in these ways but in others no one disclosed beforehand.

As it happens, Simon's music, for which he received $50,000, consists entirely of three snatches of barely audible melody, the first of which comes one hour into the film; and the writing is obvious and unpolished when considered in view of *Chinatown* and some of Towne's other work. Christie is competent but hardly memorable, and Beatty, whose performance is the backbone of the film, is somewhat shaky in this departure from what he has done in the past. The kind of actor who evolves slowly and steadily, he gives a good showing but one different from what probably was expected by audiences who have followed him in *The Parallax View*, *McCabe and Mrs. Miller* and *Bonnie and Clyde*, back through the underrated *Mickey One* and into the crowded darkness of the late 1950s.

While the essence of the film is in fact germane to the noisy politicking used as a backdrop, it has more to do with the 1960s generically than that aspect of 1960s life specifically. In this way, *Shampoo* is not merely curious and entertaining but special. It is the first meaningful 1960s film, neither a period nor a nostalgia piece, but something akin to a tiny reassessment.

The story in brief is that of a Beverly Hills hairdresser named George (Beatty), who thinks it is his job he is bored with when it is really his life. Hoping to better himself, he applies to a bank for capital with which to open his own salon, but is refused when his dishevelled appearance and vocabulary conflict with the banker's.

He then turns for the money to Jack Warden, who plays an entre-preneur with ambitions within the Republican Party. As it hap-pens, Warden's mistress, Christie, is Beatty's old girlfriend. In the course of this story, which is set against the election of Richard Nixon and Spiro Agnew in 1968, Beatty not only renews his *affaire* with Christie but also becomes involved with Warden's wife (played by Lee Grant) and daughter. All this while, Beatty is also occupied with his present girlfriend, played with wide-eyed superciliousness by Goldie Hawn.

Superficially, this would call to mind Michael Caine's 1967 role in *Alfie*, but the differences between the two characters are quite pronounced. Alfie was a satyriasis case who used his ailment to treat the larger problems of loneliness and insecurity. He at least pretended to enjoy what he was doing. But Beatty is a hapless, almost accidental sort of lecher who falls among these women all at once when his inverted moral apathy triumphs over his knowl-edge of what's good for him. He would enjoy what he is doing, or at least would be exhilarated by the danger of it, were it not for the fact that he is detached from it. It is not that he is schizophrenic so much as that he's possessed by some spirit of the 1960s, a condi-tion for which no exorcism rite exists in the *Book of Common Prayer*. It is in this attitude, it seems to me, rather than in musical, tonsorial or political detail, that *Shampoo* is a 1960s film and in that it is important.

That it is a 1960s film rather than a film made during or merely about the 1960s is an important distinction. Except for those atro-cious ones aimed at the youth market, 1960s films were not in the main conscious of being 1960s films, though inevitably some ap-peared which summed up something of the mood of the time. One thinks of *Alfie, Morgan!* and *The Graduate* when trying to recall what the 1960s felt like; these and *Midnight Cowboy*, which was made later from the novel published in 1965. *Shampoo* as far as I am aware is the first film to succeed in recapturing that mood in light of the present. Hence the election is used to point up the obvious yet unconsidered prescience of the black 1970s that existed back then. And hence Beatty has had to give a performance radically different from any he has given before.

Beatty is one of those actors who came to prominence in the early 1960s playing bored young men with a talent for apprehended out-rage. He was one who seemed to interpret Stanislavsky's ideas mainly in terms of indistinct speech. His whole career had been

51

devoted to the portrayal of one cool character, and the intensity he brought to acting jobs seldom varied more than a few degrees. While all this is recognisable in his portrayal of the hairdresser, it is combined here with a sort of ragamuffin comedy no one knew till now he was capable of, which is the essence of the role.

We are coming to think of the 1960s as having been a time of uncontrolled social energy resulting in a special kind of fatigue among the participants, and Beatty here assumes a stance related to those late-silent, early-talkies comedians who exuded such sadness and pathos. He never actually resorts to pratfalls but he looks as though he is always about to. That's how understated his performance is. That's how much he is under the weight of the world around him, this continuous circus he doesn't realise he is a part of. Whereas in earlier films his mumble was a symbol of defiance and disaffiliation, here it is a sign of imminent defeat. In *Shampoo* Beatty's mumble is a comic gesture. He mumbles the way Oliver Hardy played with his necktie or the way Chaplin tipped his hat to strangers — to show that he is just a little guy caught up in circumstances he'd laugh about if he weren't so close to tears.

Shampoo would have us believe that it makes a more serious political statement than it actually does. What it does do is to use the political theme to mix the film's two flavours, sweet and sour. It is very much a film of good scenes rather than a satisfying whole, and the two best scenes illustrate this binding technique. In the first, Warden has asked Beatty to escort his, Warden's, mistress to a campaign dinner, so as not to arouse the suspicions of Warden's wife, who will also be present. The older man warns Beatty not to let Christie drink too much, unaware of Beatty's past involvement with her. Hawn, who is rankled at not being on Beatty's arm, turns up too, on someone else's. Suspecting the truth, Warden's wife acts bitchily toward Christie, who responds in kind — and also by getting looped. The meeting of the five principals begins in great awkwardness and ends in chaos, with Christie sexually assaulting Beatty under the banquet table. All this while some politician is rambling through a partisan address of great pomposity and little meaning.

In the other scene, Warden arrives at Christie's house the next morning with two thugs, intent on having Beatty, who is there alone, worked over. But when he looks at Beatty he sees only a reflection of himself. Both are conscious of getting older while the mean age of Americans is getting lower. Both are uncertain how long they can continue to muster the energy necessary to maintain their holding actions against a society too impersonal, too fast, too corrupt in a basic sense, for them to handle. Warden's villainous impulses quickly vanish, and the two commiserate with each other, talking, if not man to man, then nebbish to nebbish. It's a very moving scene. As it unfolds, Nixon and Agnew babble callously on a television screen in the corner.

Making a film that so clearly delineates a mood, a feeling, a nuance — in short, an ontological film — is no easy matter. The temptation from this short distance would be to make instead a film labelling itself 1960s by playing up still further the already established pop images of the period. Most films to be made on the 1960s likely will do what, for example, Raoul Walsh's *The Roaring Twenties*, made in 1939, did with the 1920s: concentrate on accessories and actions and leave the responses alone.

That *Shampoo* is so successful at what it does (or so unsuccessful at what it seemed to be touted as doing) may have something to do with its appearance at the proper historical and psychological moment. Never before have we been so melancholy, and never has it been so simple, given the strength, to recapture the 1960s now that some of the cultural chaff has fallen away without damaging the grain. Yet I think *Shampoo* is the product of more than good timing. It is an uneven but subtle investigation of the way we were briefly but for whatever reasons no longer are. It will be thought of in remembering how it was back then as well as in trying to determine where we went wrong. Sure, Nixon and Agnew are useful symbols of whatever this was. But the performance of Beatty, and to a lesser extent those of Warden and Christie, are better ones. The characters they portray voted for the bastard by default, voted in favour of the 1970s and against the 1960s, and ended up at a wake instead of a celebration.

June 1975

53

Woody Guthrie became a legend rather late in his own time. In his heyday around the Second World War he was most often mistaken for a hillbilly singer on the order of Hawkshaw Hawkins. Resistance to this idea was kept alive mainly by Pete Seeger and a few other folksingers once Guthrie was no longer personally able to discourage it. Then in the early 1960s Bob Dylan began imitating the structure of Guthrie's music as a means of learning composition, the way Berg copied Schoenberg. At the same time he adopted a close approximation of Guthrie's voice and public manner. Dylan shot to fame and Guthrie became a legend on his coattails. He came to be seen as an almost mythical figure from the distant past. Despite the content of his songs, it was only then that Guthrie was recognised as the quintessential Depression-era wanderer.

Partly because of this curious distortion of time, and partly because he had been confined to hospital since 1954, Guthrie was spoken of in the especially reverent tones saved for those who die young, before their talent catches up with their potential or their actions with their principles. Actually, though, he did not die until 1967, when he was fifty-five. He was a victim of Huntington's chorea, a hereditary degenerative disease of the nervous system, for which no cure is known.

The peculiar circumstances of Guthrie's reputation, then, must have presented certain problems for Robert Getchell, who wrote the screenplay *Bound for Glory* from Guthrie's 1943 autobiography of the same title, and for Hal Ashby, the film's director. Their initial temptation must have been to make the standard musician's story, the kind beginning with the subject's acquisition of his first instrument and following through with various tragedies and career highlights. The Hollywood biopic as a form, however, has never been well suited to the depiction of artists, who must spend the best part of their lives inside their own heads. Often such films are thinly disguised musicals, as was the case recently with Gordon Park's *Leadbelly*. Wisely, Getchell and Ashby forgot all the precedents and made a film that panders unashamedly to the legend that Guthrie the man saw being created from his hospital bed. *Bound for Glory* makes no pretense of being a biography, a musical or a propaganda film. It's not *really* about Woody Guthrie or what he did and stood for in his own time. It's about the way many people today like to think of him.

One good indication of this approach is the casting of David Carradine as Guthrie. Carradine, who in the past has always seemed to me to have behaved as though in a Roger Corman movie, is here suitably understated, as though aware of having only to confirm, not challenge, our image of Guthrie. Similarly, the script covers only four years of Guthrie's life, from 1936 to 1940, before the war and career demands brought him east, away from the dustbowl states and the northwest with which many of his songs are concerned. While the whole film is wonderfully evocative of the time and place, and while care has been taken with locations and properties (allowing for some suspiciously recent-looking steel boxcars), the film is not a period piece, for one is not struck throughout by the authenticity of such things. Rather, it is one of those films in which the subject himself defines the period in our memory. In the popular imagination, Guthrie dominates the time and the locale the way Dr. Johnson does late eighteenth-century London. The memory of the personality is in sharper focus than the surroundings.

In Arthur Penn's film of *Alice's Restaurant*, starring Guthrie's son Arlo as himself, there was a scene in which, beating a retreat through some slum or other, Arlo paused long enough to say, "Looks like Woody could have passed through here." *Bound for Glory* has no such coyness but is quite concerned with the spirit of that remark. The first half hour is spent setting the scene for Guthrie's vagabondage by instilling in us the sense of hopelessness he must have felt. Born in Oklahoma, he was at that time living in Pampa, Texas, earning a living of sorts as a signpainter. When the droughts made nature and the economy seem in collusion, he like so many others simply struck out for what promised to be a better life in California. In doing so, he left behind his wife and children (Arlo was borne by a later wife, the official widow, who is not referred to in the film).

Basically what transpires is that the rough journey radicalises him, and he begins creating songs as an outlet for his emotional disquiet. Later, he takes up with a recruiter for the farmworkers' union (modelled apparently on Cisco Houston) and himself becomes a singing activist. When his songs come to the attention of the commercial music business, he compromises only so far. Time and again he sticks his foot in the mouth of opportunity, even to the detriment of his family, with whom he is now for a time reunited. All the supporting actors, such as Randy Quaid as an Okie and Ronny Cox as the labour organiser, handle themselves well. There are even one or two rousing moments, as when at a strike meeting Guthrie sings his composition "Union Maid," which to my certain knowledge was sung in similar situations as recently as a dozen years ago.

Bound for Glory is in some ways nostalgia for what we never knew and what probably never existed in such simplicity. Guthrie, for instance, comes across as a fellow who suffered fools gladly enough but had a blanket disorder with anyone from some other class. But the realization of that fact is as far as the film ever goes in discussing his politics. The reason for this reticence, perhaps, is that upon close inspection his politics were not what befit the legend. Guthrie was a left liberal (he campaigned for FDR and accepted songwriting commissions from the New Deal) who was made to seem farther left by the turmoil that surrounded him in his prime. It is true that sometimes he claimed to be a communist, but in truth and to his credit, he was the type of communist who always gets kicked out of the party for having sense of humour. The film, like the legend, is careful not to alienate anyone by delving too deeply even into this point. Perhaps that accounts for some of the movie's strong appeal.

The 1930s of our collective imagination is politicized and polarized almost unto frustration. Guthrie's attractiveness in such a context is that he was not Mike Gold or Max Eastman but a person whose beliefs sprang totally from instinctive humanism. Guthrie was no intellectual, he was never heard arguing some fine point of Spanish anarcho-syndicalism, and it is unlikely that he ever met anyone remotely connected with the London School of Economics. His ideas and for the most part his songs were concerned ultimately with the quality of daily life (usually his own), not the ownership of the means of production. His politics were either rough-hewn Christianity or touching naïveté, depending upon one's own. At any event, the overwhelming preponderance of Americans found themselves (as they probably would today) at least marginally more in sympathy with him than at hazard. In 1939, it was hard not to like someone who pasted to his guitar a sign reading THIS MACHINE KILLS FASCISTS. In the 1970s, it's difficult to dislike his shade for the additional reason that such a person is now a symbol of his generation.

By far the most remarkable aspect of *Bound for Glory*, however, is Haskell Wexler's cinematography. It is especially appealing when considered in tandem with the editing by Robert Jones and Pembroke J. Herring and the special effects by Saas Bedig, who have been too little acknowledged. In 1963 it was fashionable to say that F.A. Young's camera work on David Lean's *Lawrence of Arabia* was so good that one came away from the theatre parched and dusty. To my mind, the statement can be applied more accurately here. For quite a while we are treated to the little Texas town that is literally blowing away day by day. Then we are given an aerial shot of a special (but not optional) effect: a huge cloud of dust many storeys high sweeping in. The scene was created simply by blowing forty tons of loose dirt with aeroplane engines. It is evidence that the simple ways are oftentimes better than the expensive and exotic ones: a fact filmmakers seem to have forgotten recently. Was there ever a more realistic battle scene than the Confederate infantry charge in *The Birth of a Nation*, or a simpler one? Griffith, not having access to today's advanced technology and retrograde ideas, simply dressed up thousands of extras in period uniforms and had them, on signal, charge across a wide expanse of field at a single camera.

Wexler is one of the most accomplished cinematographers around today and is becoming the best known, and with cause. His adaptability is what is most striking. Cameramen of the past made their reputations through sheer longevity (as did James Wong Howe) or, in a few cases, through a more or less consistent overall technique (as did Lee Garmes). Wexler, however, seems to discard past styles and begin afresh with each film. For Jewison's *The Thomas Crown Affair*, for instance, he produced crisp, orderly and artificially bright footage that lent contemporaneousness to the story. Later, in *Who's Afraid of Virginia Woolf?*, his style was tighter, grainier and at times a little woozy, in harmony with the characters. Here he relies on earth colours but shies from graininess, so as to reconfirm that the film has a Depression background but is not a historical picture. His mobility is just as interesting. He gets inside the storyline, sometimes by shooting from what seems to the vantage point of some unseen friend of a second or third character. His establishing shots never look like establishing shots, and he does not appear to be shooting sets even when he is in fact doing precisely that.

It is ironic that the success of *Bound for Glory* will probably steer him even farther away from directing — a field he abandoned after only one film, the remarkable *Medium Cool*. His name is now very prominent indeed in the credits as photographer. The real irony of *Bound for Glory*, though, is that there's no credit to Bob Dylan. He

57

is truly the person (as Oscar recipients are given to say) without whom none of this would have happened.

June – July 1977

◆

It's strangely difficult to realize that the war in Viet Nam has been over for little more than three years, not a decade as would seem to be the case. This realisation is not on the whole displeasing but it's hard to achieve. One wants to forget the entire mess without letting the villains forget it. One longs to consign the era to history while retaining censorship rights over history's interpretations. So we act as though the war is past but keep calling up images of it. We call them up, I fear, mainly to allow ourselves the luxury of weariness. The result is an anarchic distortion of time. One book on the war and American movies has already been remaindered for God's sake, even though the important fictional films on the subject (practically the only ones, in fact) have just now begun appearing. This illustrates a curious situation that may also be connected with the failure at the time of an instant pop culture to deal adequately with circumstances that simply refused to go away. We want to forget but also remember. We are angry that we can't do both at once.

Or such is the source of at least some of the hostility and disappointment aroused by Hal Ashby's *Coming Home*, which has beaten both *Apocalypse Now* and *Dog Soldiers* to the screen. The rest springs from the film's muddled viewpoint and from some artistic problems, many of which result from pre-production difficulties. The film was made military fashion. Jane Fonda conceived the project more than six years ago when she was still in the public's bad graces for visiting the North. She hired Nancy Dowd to write it but they quarreled over the result. Dowd's credit was reduced to that of "story by" and the script was thoroughly overhauled by the bankable Waldo Salt. This version in turn was redone by Robert C. Jones, presumably with Fonda and by this time Ashby looking over his shoulder. Certainly Ashby's personal style is visible throughout the film in more than the direction alone. *Coming Home* in fact can easily be seen as a sister film to *Shampoo*. Many of the technical preferences are the same. Also, both are set in Southern California in 1968 and both are anti-war in flavour though they deal only with the home front (curiously, to see anything of the Vietnamese people one must go back to John Wayne's *Green Berets*).

Ashby's director of photography here is Haskell Wexler. Everyone seems to have forgotten that they first worked together on *The Loved One* in 1965, which Ashby cut and Wexler not only shot but co-produced. Instead, they're remembered as a team from *Bound for Glory*, on which they seemed more in sync. Here, as before, Wexler's photography is remarkable for its appropriateness to the time and space; he captures that chronic forced gaiety of Southern California weather and the effect upon various colours of sunlight filtered through smog. Ashby, though, seems at odds with much of the material, principally because the characters simply aren't developed as they should be. In terms of the script, in fact, the three major figures are so many stock characters, uniformly familiar. It's the different depths of the actors, and also our political sympathy with some of their parts, that make them work.

Fonda plays the career wife of a career Marine played by Bruce Dern. Temperamentally and theoretically he's a staunch hawk eager for the opportunity to be one in actual practice as well. Dern, whose acting has seldom been as arresting as his face, even in *The King of Marvin Gardens*, looks the part but opts for making the character maniacal. Anyway, with her husband away in the war, Fonda volunteers to help the wounded in a veterans' hospital as a way of passing the time. The experience brings about important changes in her. It radicalises her, or at least prepares her emotionally for opposing the war retroactively. It provides the circumstances for her falling in love with Jon Voight, an old school mate who's come home a paraplegic. The two happenings are of course interconnected on many levels and with several ramifications. Her husband's simple absence means the opportunity to meet Voight, whose condition turns her against the war and inevitably against her husband as well. This is the heart of the film, but despite several powerful scenes and much skilful filmmaking, we simply don't get a very strong evocation of all these necessary emotions. Why, that's Jane Fonda up there and we're just supposed to know from reading the papers how she feels in such a situation. And Dern, well, he's that insulting stereotype of made-for-TV movies, the Viet Nam vet who's gone crazy, whose actions aren't really his own, whose condition is not *our* fault, no, but society's. Nonsense.

59

About the time *Coming Home* was released I was talking with a screenwriter friend of mine who'd been brought in to redo a script for one of the expatriate Canadian directors. The story was about this crippled Viet Nam veteran returning home. "I was two drafts in the job and working on the third," my friend told me. "When the Fonda movie appeared I feared the worst, expecting to go down for the third instalment of the fee and find a family of gipsies living in the office." But instead of shying from the competition, the producer was delighted with *Coming Home*. "We're pushing ahead," my friend reported, "because he now thinks that paraplegic chic is going to be big." An amazing point of view even from a money-grubbing producer but a useful one if it makes you question just what *Coming Home* is in fact about. It's not about the war, I think now, in the sense that so much music and so many of the dominant films of just a few years ago were. Those films dealt implicitly with the great moral propositions of the war: films such as Wexler's *Medium Cool*, Schlesinger's *Midnight Cowboy*, Ashby's *Shampoo*, which were every bit as clear a response to the war as, say, 1920s novels were to the First World War. *Coming Home*, by comparison, is closer to those First World War anti-war features made in the 1930s. It uses the war as a metaphor for domestic crises instead of the other way around.

The difference is not so much one of intent as of distance. The film is at times incredibly moving not because of any immediacy but because it arouses in us passions, resentments, feelings of fatigue, a whole boatload of emotions we don't want to relive. It's an easy film to dislike oneself for seeing if one isn't ready yet to begin reading the autobiographies of one's own generation, which one most decidedly is not.

Then, too, there are other arguments pro and con. The film is gripping also because of some of the performances. Penelope Milford is marvelous as Fonda's friend and neighbour. Fonda is restrained and purposeful but too naturalistic. There's no I-told-you-so attitude in her performance. John Voight (who was fourth choice for the part after Sylvester Stallone, Jack Nicholson and Al Pacino) is more the activist. He's also the central actor in the whole enterprise, though he goes in here for whites and blacks to set off Fonda's shading. On the minus side, however, is the fact that the filmmaking is not always up to what one would expect in an ambitious Ashby project. Sometimes the problem is staleness. In scenes where the plot turns coincide with emotional peaks, the film is redolent of many other movies before it. And where it should duplicate past successes it doesn't. The Dern figure, for instance, isn't informed by the same sort of military believability as the characters in *The Last Detail*. Also, Ashby takes some very cheap shots indeed in the editing and mixing. Here as in *Shampoo* he uses songs of 1968 — Dylan, the Stones and others — on the soundtrack. In this case, though, the lyrics are often an ironic comment on the concurrent action. In the same manner, he cuts from Marines running in battle to the wounded crawling in hospital.

These cumulative annoyances simply erupt when the script begins to falter: when the husband confronts his wife and her lover, the thing fizzles. The husband has gone crazy, unconvincingly, and later drowns himself. The story lingers on the two survivors longer than it should, through one redundant scene after another, to tug at the old heart strings. It's as though Ashby wanted to *neutralise* the war in our memories. Perhaps this is why the film is so easy to take argument with, despite many nice flourishes not even mentioned here.

Either one wants to forget the war entirely or to remember its lessons. One doesn't want someone saying it was nicer or more romantic or even less complicated than it was — not unless you're a veteran who's into the simple nostalgia of *The Boys in Company C*. Yet a sense of such auto-exorcism is exactly what one gets from seeing Fonda and Voight on the screen. They're irritating in this context if for no other reason than they're long in the tooth. One of the points, surely, is that the people caught up in the war buggered up their lives for good when they were seventeen, eighteen, twenty, twenty-one. To see these forty-year-olds explaining the pain with footnotes to a new generation, and either getting it wrong or not telling the whole truth, is mildly disquieting if not objectionable. Or such is the common feeling at present. A decade from now the film will have probably lost most of its impact. Its flaws will be either more or less obvious, whereas ten years *ago* they wouldn't have mattered as they do now. That was the time to have made such a film. The problem was not that people wouldn't have listened. The problem was that nobody had the guts when the chips were down.

April 1978

III

Paul Mazursky's *Next Stop, Greenwich Village* appears to be something it is not. It looks to be the first feature of a quite talented new director, the equivalent in mood and texture of, for instance, Martin Scorsese's *Mean Streets*. Actually, though, it's neither that nor the logical result of Mazursky's previous films such as *Blume in Love* and *Bob & Carol & Ted & Alice*. The reason the film seems to be what it isn't has to do with the fact that Mazursky has discarded slickness for the type of carefully distilled personal statement commonly found in the work of brilliant newcomers. In this case, the personal statement is one with absorbing sociological and historical implications. The film, as the title makes plain, is about the Greenwich Village experience so important as a symbol in the cultural life of the United States.

For the better part of a century now the Village has occupied in the minds of the American intelligentsia the place occupied in the minds of the rest of the nation by the frontier or in the minds of Canadians by the CBC. That is to say, it has always been in decline. No matter what period of wild west history one looks at one finds nostalgia for the way it had been a short time earlier, before the coming of the automobile, the railway or the settlers with their devil-wire. And so on back into time. The Village has been like this too.

The persons who now occupy SoHo (as the Bowery has come to be called) look back fondly to the early 1960s when people such as Dylan lived in the Village proper. Survivors of that epoch in turn look back to the Village of the 1950s with its Beats who, it follows, thought highly of the radical Village of the 1930s. The *New Masses* people, of course, got misty over John Reed and the days of Mabel Dodge. There is about the Village a sense that the grass is always greener on the other side of the grave. There has always been a sense that one was taking part in a fine, sad tradition: the Oxford of the self-educated. *Next Stop* is partly about this phenomenon; or at least its characters are set against this background. The characters are Lenny Baker as Larry Lapinsky (who is clearly some previous incarnation of Mazursky himself) and Ellen Greene as his girlfriend Sarah.

The scene is Brooklyn in 1953. Lapinsky is an aspiring twenty-two-year-old actor whose reason for leaving home is a compound of his motives in wanting to. He first of all wants to be with a family of peers rather than a family of parents. At least he wants to be free of his strident Jewish mother (Shelley Winters) who is selfishly concerned with his welfare instead of his wishes. This desire for peers is associated with both his struggles to be an actor and his passion for Sarah, of whom his mother would disapprove (as indeed she would of any woman he might take up with). This situation brings about in him something like schizophrenia which, if it is his burden as a private person, is also, eventually, his charm as an actor. It leaves him with a talent for (one could almost say an addiction to) flippant comedy. He escapes, at will, into a kind of verbal mischief, impersonating Brando, cutting up and generally cracking wise. There is, I believe, a message here from Mazursky, the failed actor become director: that what is cheap in real life can be gold on stage; that a performer's triumphs are really inversions of his or her personal shortcomings. It's an old idea but one that underlies the film's structure and its comedy.

Next Stop, Greenwich Village has a plot all right but it is a weak and overworked one. Sarah, inevitably, becomes pregnant by Larry and has an abortion: two events one sees coming right from the start. There is also a certain amount of emotional hanky-panky among Lapinsky's contemporaries and, off-camera, some of the physical kind as well. Dramatically the film is much too stagy, in the literal sense, with characters entering and exiting at neatly timed intervals. The film is like a sixth draft script that's supposed to be seamless but isn't by the very fact of its constant revision. This fault is especially apparent in the unevenness of the dialogue. Like the main character, the movie has its strength not in its deliberate seriousness but in its frequent moments of offhand comedy. In those terms, it is first-rate, with memorable bits of business and many little deflations of youthful pretension.

Indeed, this is in every way a film about a certain stage of youth, a film not so much about loss of innocence as acquisition of responsibility. When, at the end, Lapinsky makes what appears to be a very positive screen test, we know that he is soon off to the West Coast. We know that he will spend the rest of his days, which will be very busy, lamenting the loss of the Village atmosphere. He will go on recalling the time when his ambition and drive seem, in retrospect, to have been at odds with his not having to get up in the morning if he didn't bloody well feel like it. Although this is film about youth from the point of view of youth, its critical and nostalgic tone tells us that it is made from maturity. The maturity is also evident in the construction.

Mazursky uses (probably overuses) the technique of lingering on a scene once the main character or characters have left the shot. Most other directors use this trick to build up a sense of setting that might otherwise be lost to viewers concentrating on the principals. Some directors, I would wager, even do this to test themselves, to reassure themselves as well as the audience that the animate and inanimate parts of the film are in harmony. Mazursky, however, seems to do so because his photographic loitering lets him exhibit his fine cast of supporting characters, which includes such ancient Village types as an elegant black homosexual and a woman who keeps trying to kill herself and finally succeeds. By allowing each of these people one big moment in the afterglow of the narrative he makes them seem more integral than they are. A less noble reason is that the technique lets the director indulge himself in his own nostalgia. It allows him to remember for a few more seconds, the audience be damned, just what it was like in that place and that time, when he was young. This would explain why, at one point, he lingers just a bit too long on an empty room. Such are the dangers of reviving, for commercial purposes, a personal experience which is not yet completely digested.

Yet the personal aspect is the saving grace of the film as well as its failing. Mazursky is relating, within clearly stated bounds of geography and class, the early 1950s as he knew them. He is making something on the order of a 1950s *American Graffiti*, a film this one resembles in texture and approach. He is being general by being specific and by presenting a case history. So it is that the sexual elements of the film work quite well. Sexually, his characters are bored, selfish, naïve and just generally wrong headed and screwed up. In that way they seem to ring true to one's conception of 1953. It is only when he seeks to lay on the period with a trowel, with too many references to the Rosenberg executions and to McCarthy, that he breaks the spell of authenticity.

The spell-breaking — the reversion to the old Hollywood notion that accuracy of reference constitutes true authenticity — is also apparent insofar as the film relates directly to Greenwich Village. It's true that the spirit of the area is well captured and disseminated. Mazursky relates with skill the contentment that comes with incorporating into one's life, as mock-truths, the accumulated misconceptions of the ages, the way Villagers have done for decades.

64

But this only leads to bursting the bubble for the part of the audience familiar with the folklore of the place.

Early in the film, when Lapinsky and the others are lounging in an unmistakably Village bar, there appears a wizened, white-bearded old fellow hawking his poems. He reads one of them, to wit: "In winter I'm a buddhist, In summer I'm a nudist." The couplet of course is the work of Joe Gould, the 1920s leftover who spent his days (Joseph Mitchell and the *New Yorker* notwithstanding) writing his unfinished Oral History of the World. The characterization is unmistakable. The actor, a present day Village character known only as Maurice, is a Gould lookalike and the verse is Gould's best known (not best) contribution to Village eccentricity. What's disturbing is that the character is referred to as Jake. Thereafter one keeps expecting old Max Bodenheim to turn up as well, cadging drinks. One dreads the prospect because the likelihood is that he will be distorted in the same way.

The Joe Gould scene is only a brief one. But thinking about it one imagines Mazursky with memos from lawyers warning of possible claims by the estate of Gould, who died in 1957. It creates early on a sour taste which keeps recurring days later in explanations of why *Next Stop, Greenwich Village* fails to live up to the promise it uses only to tease. Although a moving film and a poignant one, and more interestingly put together than it seems at first — despite these things and all the rest, it is, even in the penultimate analysis, hokey. That is to say that Hollywood triumphs, from the grave, so to speak. Hollywood and the Village are mythologically similar in that they both encourage the taking on of other generations' pretensions.

April 1976

◆

Richard Corliss has written that Paul Mazursky is among those new directors who have brought to U.S. cinema "a vaguely European concern" with individual character studies. Corliss went on to say that while "most of the others (Robert Altman, Alan J. Pakula, Hal Ashby, Martin Scorsese) are interested in the behavioral extremes," Mazursky deals with the middle ground. "Give Altman a handful of All-American flakes, and he'll end up with a shootup or a breakdown; give Scorsese the story of a bebop musician, and he'll turn it into *psychopathia sexualis*." One can agree that Mazursky is different if not with the explanation Corliss offers. Mazursky is different all right. Mazursky is boring.

He's boring mainly because he doesn't have much truth to tell us. In his new film *An Unmarried Woman*, an array of characters are made to seem cardboard so that the main one, played by Jill Clayburgh, will stand out in high relief. Clayburgh does her job well enough but ultimately the film doesn't go anywhere. The use to which the cardboard is put emphasizes that Mazursky's films are characterised by a certain insincerity. They're slick, frequently funny, oftentimes penetrating in small details, but not convincing. One enters into a Mazursky film knowing that it's going to be the moviegoing equivalent of those people at parties who try masking their glibness by telling you how honest their relationships are.

If this sounds too harsh, I'd like to believe it's only because ridiculing *An Unmarried Woman* is almost as instructive as it is easy. Clayburgh plays a character named Erica. She's in her mid-thirties, married to a stockbroker and lives in an antiseptic apartment on the East Side of New York. She keeps in shape. She's involved. She travels with a circle of friends who are either less secure than herself or simply more forthright. Two other pertinent facts about Erica are that her husband is an ass of incredible callowness and that she works part-time in a gallery, being a serious patroniser of the arts. The point is that for the most part apparently she's happy and contented. Until.

One day her husband (played by Michael Murphy) picks her up for lunch. Afterwards with no very great conviction, he bursts into tears in the middle of Spring Street. He tells her that he's leaving her for another woman, whom he fell in love with a year earlier at the shirt counter at Bloomingdale's. Erica walks away haughtily. Once out of his sight, she throws up. For a time she is understandably loath to see other men. She does have one date, however, with a press agent who looks like Clive Davis, but she becomes uncontrollable ablewhen he tries to kiss her in the back of a taxi. When even her family doctor makes a passive move on her — well. But subsequently, on the advice of Tania, her shrink, whom we are led to believe is gay, she seeks male companionship. First she has a fling with an obnoxious cryptoartist but backs off when he becomes affectionate. This is a sign of her growing independence. Then at a party she meets another artist, a raffish Alan Bates type (played by Alan Bates). This is a character without faults who's at times almost as cardboardy in his beefcake sensitivity as the husband had been in his unglamorous reserve. He wants her to go away with him for the summer. She resists, having found the strength and confidence she never knew she possessed, or something.

The film has elements of previous Mazursky films but in a poor combination. There's the attention to vacuous minutiae one finds in *Bob & Carol & Ted & Alice*, his first film as a director. The difference is that Mazursky then was peeping through the keyhole of those laid-back California pretenders to whom ancient wisdom has been reduced to so much pop psychology. He was directing as a skeptical easterner, close enough to conversion for danger but cynical enough not to be taken in. In *An Unmarried Woman*, by contrast, he actually seems to take his characters on faith. Doing so is made easier by the fact that Clayburgh looks like a real person, not like an actress. She shows enviable self-control in keeping from smirking as much as Diane Keaton does, and to date she's not so well known that we're always conscious of her being a star first and the character second. Even so, it's mistaken for Mazursky to imagine that the recognition factor of Erica will compensate for this film's failure to develop. It's almost as though he believes that this movie is somehow more serious than some Neil Simon play simply because it contains less comedy. It's as though he believes he is telling us pleasant or unpleasant truths about ourselves merely by giving a slick product a little texture.

This texture in Mazursky's films is always deserving of attention, though, and it's achieved in a variety of ways, not all of them easy to pinpoint. Each movie has one or two short scenes or pieces of business that strike one as perfect to the mood if superfluous to the story. In *Next Stop, Greenwich Village*, which was set in 1953, there was the scene in which everyone joined a conga line to slither merrily through street traffic. In *An Unmarried Woman* there's a marvelous bit, equally unimportant in itself but useful as a bridge, in which Erica and her fifteen-year-old daughter (Lisa Lucas) play a McCartney song together on the piano. Then there's the extent to which the city itself is a character in Mazursky films. *Next Stop*, being autobiographical and historical, treated New York nostalgically but with restraint. Mazursky had known the West Village intimately and remembered it clearly. SoHo represents a different generation and is a different matter entirely. He concentrates too much on specific locations and street names as though trying to convince us of his familiarity with an ethos that's not mirrored very well on the screen. *An Unmarried Woman* has no grit. His lofts look too much like penthouses, his tenements too much like apartment buildings.

Much of the mood and much of what's objectionable in the film come from the cinematographic style and from the editing. As in *Bob & Carol & Ted & Alice*, he takes a documentary approach at times, though more subtly here than previously, with less good reason and to worse effect. Medium shots become slow zooms-in and slow zooms-out, all in one smooth motion, as though this were italicizing something important being said. The trouble is that nothing important *is* being said; the shots are just television tricks. Similarly, there are too many scenes that begin with waist-up shots of the subject's back in the lower right-hand part of the frame when the subject's opening lines are already on the soundtrack. A related device is the conversation in which we hear a line or two of Person A's monotonal candid-camera-like dialogue while the camera is still on a tight shot of expressionless Person B, whose eyes are glazed. These are all techniques to seduce us subliminally into believing that *An Unmarried Woman* is some sort of docudrama, a slice of life and therefore meaningful.

Don't get me wrong. It's not a disagreeable film. It's simply a case of Mazursky failing to do more than put a few kinks on his stereotypes. The same story, the same feel, has been better put across before in such films as *Diary of a Mad Housewife*. It's true that the theme is a basic one always in need of retelling: the man and the woman who find each other emotional and practical at the wrong times, who grow apart and perhaps become better as a consequence. In the hands of someone without the right equipment, however, it can never come out fresh, only slick. This unequal ratio of slickness to guts is not quite the same problem Fred Zinnemann faced recently in *Julia*. Zinnemann was trying to adhere to the text, which was one of the stories in Lillian Hellman's *Pentimento*. As the title of the book would suggest, the story was structurally too slight for the more bombastic medium. But Mazursky was not so bound. He was free as always to make his own film. As usual, he thought that by slipping in and out of several motifs and making rough edges of plaster of paris he could compensate for not getting his hands dirty. It didn't work. Clayburgh holds the film together better than Erica holds her life together, but then Erica is a cartoon woman (though one of the better sort). With filmmakers as with novelists, there are those who deal with people, those who deal only with themselves and those who are mainly artifice. Where Mazursky falls I'm not quite sure, but it's not in the same league as Ashby and Scorsese.

June – July 1978

Archetypes

I

Dear Dick Richards,

I have just come from seeing the picture you've made of my book *Farewell, My Lovely*. Let me tell you right off the bat that I like it. I have not liked many of the pictures that have come out since my death. I wasn't too crazy about most of the older ones either. I always liked a good murder yarn but most of the ones I saw were set in England somewhere. They were all about the poisoning of Her Nibs the Duchess of So-and-so. They did not appeal to me. Such pictures are full of pansies and they have butlers in them and they keep reminding me of my own Englishness which I wasted a life trying to forget. I like pictures about broken-down private dicks and coppers and jokers on the skids. Since my death I have not seen many of these, as I say. But I saw yours. I like it. This letter is to say thanks, pal.

I like many things about your picture. The thing I like best is Robert

Mitchum. He's not exactly what I had in mind with Philip Marlowe but he's pretty close. For one thing he's a little long in the tooth. I first made Marlowe up in *The Big Sleep*. This was published in 1939. *Farewell, My Lovely* was the second time I used him. I wrote this book in 1940 and set it in the same year. At this time Marlowe was still on the shy side of thirty-five. At tops, thirty-five. Mitchum is fifty-five if he's a day and most likely he's pushing sixty. But he's got the right build and pretty much the right kind of face.

As you know Marlowe has been played in pictures before. The first one to play him was George Sanders in *The Falcon Takes Over* in 1942. Well, it sure as hell wasn't my idea. Then in a couple years along came Dick Powell. I didn't think much of this either. Dick Powell was a hoofer before he was an actor and in the first version of *Farewell, My Lovely* he looked like a hoofer playing a private eye. I kept expecting him to start dancing up some alley like it was a musical. I don't like musicals and never did. Neither did Marlowe. Robert Montgomery played Marlowe too. This was in *The Lady in the Lake*. He wasn't bad but he wasn't too good. Then there was James Garner. He had the build for it but he had a hair-do like some homo. Marlowe had hair on his head all right but it was there to soak up the blood.

The last time round for Marlowe was in *The Long Goodbye* by this Altman character. Altman can't tell a story. He doesn't know much about actors either. In this picture Marlowe was played by someone called Elliott Gould. Gould's a skinny little punk with curly hair who looks like a porch climber ready for the dead wagon. He was worse than the hoofer. When I saw this picture I bought a mickey and then thought about it and went out and got a fifth. As a gumshoe Gould didn't know his ass from Ventura Boulevard.

Until your picture the best Marlowe was Bogart. He was good all right but not as good as Mitchum. I knew the guy and liked him but he wasn't any Mitchum. He did time as Hammett's Sam Spade and he was okay. But when he came round to doing Marlowe he acted exactly the same. This was wrong. Spade had a slimy streak in him like a bail bondsman. Spade was a smartass. Marlowe was just a wisenheimer. There's a difference. Bogart played the same character under two different names. I didn't like this. I bet Hammett didn't like it either. Mitchum is different. Like I say, I think your picture is pretty good. I know what I'm talking about. I worked on a few pictures myself. Some people still like the stuff I did on *Double Indemnity*. They're right. It wasn't bad for what it

71

was. At least it didn't have a butler and queers running round and all that malarkey.

I like the way you put this thing together. I like the two flat feet. They're perfect. I like this dame Charlotte Rampling as Velma. She's a limey but it doesn't show. She's a little skinny and her face looks like a tooth powder ad but she's got great gams. Velma's supposed to be the kind of dame that causes guys to change their insurance policies. Your Velma is like this. She's all right.

Another think I like is that you lifted a lot of stuff from the book, you and this writer with the fag name David Zelag Goodman. Like when Marlowe tells the guy with the ransom money to stay down on the floor in the back seat. "This car stands out like spats at an Iowa picnic." I also like the Marlowe voice-over. When Moose walks up behind him in the restaurant you have Mitchum saying, "I was eating some Chinese food when a dark shadow fell over my chop suey." This is great stuff. It's some of my best writing. I'm glad you kept all this stuff in the picture. This is partly why I like it. I think you went overboard with the stuff about DiMaggio and the stuff about the Negroes. But I guess you were trying for the 1940s angle. I'm not bellyaching. I'm just telling you how it looks to me.

But this isn't mainly what I wrote to tell you. What I want to tell you is to say thanks for the way you covered for me. My faults I mean. I admit it, I got some. And also for the way you made the good parts stand out. This is what makes the thing a good picture. What I mean is I was writing about the 1940s when they were going on. I wasn't writing period stuff. I was trying to write a real detective yarn. But plots and clues and all that bunk bored the pants off me. Still do.

I was gangbusters when it came to action but not worth a tinkers damn on this other stuff. Anytime I got in a jam on the plot I'd come up with something like "He took out his roscoe and it barked." I got carried away on the action parts. I also went on a tangent on the characters. What I ended up with was sleazy writing about sleazy characters. It wasn't good mystery writing the way some of the limey stuff might be if you took out all the baloney. It wasn't even a real detective tale. The characters were just bums who were there for the atmosphere instead of the story. Besides there were too many of them. They kept standing up in the middle of the story like clarinet players. Then they'd sit back down before you could get the goods on them. Why I like your picture is because it makes me look better than I am. You didn't monkey with my book too much but you managed to not ballocks it up like I did.

I'm trying to figure how you did it. I'm trying to dope this thing out. I'm sitting here with a glass beside my Underwood Noiseless trying to figure how it worked better for you than it did for me. The bottle beside the glass is empty now. The glass is full of stale smoke. The ashtray is full of stubbed out Camels and looks like the scene of an Indian massacre.

Take those old Sherlock Holmes stories. Their plots don't make sense either when you take them apart. Not much sense anyway. No more than mine. The reason people still read that stuff is because it tells them about the way England was back then. It tells them how a part of London used to be or at least what Doyle thought it was like. Nobody reads him for the mystery. That's kid stuff. They read him for the one smart limey and all the limey creeps. They've probably got more readers now than ever because all this stuff is gone now. This makes it more interesting. My books are just the same.

I'm writing about California the same as Hammett and this other guy Macdonald. It's the capital the same way London was. People read my books to be on the inside track about what happens here. They want to keep up with the locals. They want to know more than the locals do. That's why they eat up this sleazy stuff with a spoon. It's stuff even the locals don't know about, most of them. Los Angeles is a dull burg just like London. But there's all these characters in the shadows just like London. All these old whores and muscatel winos. Nobody knows them but Marlowe. Marlowe and any joker in Nebraska with three bucks for one of my books or your show. That's why I'm popular I guess.

What makes my stuff more popular all the time is that people aren't reading it any more in the time when it was written. They aren't just out for a good yarn anymore. They're expecting 1940s stuff. It's like Holmes only American. Every Englishman thinks thirty years ago things were better. He thinks thirty years ago the rich had more dough and butlers were easier to find. He thinks it was nice and quiet then. He thinks it was easy to be smart like Holmes. He wants to think this because he liked it the way it was.

Americans believe thirty years ago the cops were tougher and the dames were easier. They think Marlowe is in the know. This is what Americans want to be instead of smart. They think it was easier to be in the know back then. They think it was a sleazier time. They want to be sleazy because that's better than what they are now. My books tell them that even LA in 1940 was sleazy. This means there's hope for them all. They forget about the mystery crap I sweated over. They fall hook, line and sinker for the stuff I produced when I was going overboard. They think I was writing the way it really was.

That's why I'm writing you, Richards. To say thanks for giving me a leg up. This scotch makes it seem like a pretty good picture. It makes my book seem better than it is. It makes LA look like a real place which it isn't and never was. I owe you one, Richards. Pick up the marker anytime.

Yours truly,

Raymond Chandler

October 1975

I I

Few films of recent years have received more ballyhoo than *Rocky*. Doubtless the advance publicity can be partly ascribed to energetic promotion men. But it is also the result of the fact that the writer of the film and the star are the same person — Sylvester Stallone — a hitherto little known actor with no writing credits whatever. Indeed, it was upon this fact that much of the publicity was based. It is sad that the film as the product of one person's imagination is in itself enough to warrant such attention. Yet the American movie business has seldom practised the individualism it preaches, and has produced relatively few convincing personal statements. In fact, allowing everything for volume, there are fewer now, in the age of the indies, than at the time of the monolithic studios. Such considerations are, I believe, important, because *Rocky* is a competent enough film in the tradition of many substandard ones. At least it starts out that way. *Rocky* wants desperately to be a film but ends up as little more than another moom pitcher. Such perhaps is the price of independence.

The Rocky of the title is a small potatoes Philadelphia boxer. At thirty he is already over the hill, though it goes without saying that at one time he could have been a contendah. The character, of course, is a favourite Hollywood stereotype, the exact male equivalent of the whore with a heart of gold. It must be said at once that no one has ever portrayed him with more texture than Stallone. Hollywood films, made for the most part by failed intellectuals, have rarely succeeded in creating major characters of selfcontained nobodies who are happy without any culture at all. Stallone, however, does so. He does so, in fact, without relying on cheap devices. He is a skilled bit actor, having appeared in, among other films, *Capone*, *The Lords of Flatbush* and, most memorably, *Farewell, My Lovely*. He is therefore close enough to the basics of dramaturgy to remember that characters must be revealed, not explained. Stallone is the star of the film in the commercial sense but his character is also the star of the story.

Since *The Champ* in 1931, most fight pictures (excepting some of the biopix) have sought to show the ring as a centre of venality and outright corruption. Some have played more upon the organised crime connection than others, but by the time of *The Harder They Fall* and *Requiem for a Heavyweight* the theme was firmly entrenched. A more recent film, John Huston's *Fat City*, failed to

75

get the notice it deserved at least partly because it refused to pander to the audience's view of fighters as either malleable children or actual hoodlums. *Rocky* owes its importance to the way it deals with a boxer in human terms; it owes its ability to do so to good timing. The stereotypes that became clichés are now receding into mere familiarity — common ground for filmmaker and audience — because corruption is now taken for granted, in sport even more than in politics. Rocky is a corrupt figure all right. Between semi-professional bouts he makes a living intimidating people for a loan shark, and later in the film, trades what integrity he can for a shot at glory in a supposedly rigged match. All that, however, is expected. The film is not an exposé. The character's morality is so much biographical information, arbitrarily supplied.

Part of the pleasure of seeing *Rocky* comes from the simplicity of the script and the production values, at least in the part of the film that establishes the character so thoroughly in our minds. The craft in this part is not so subtle that we fail to appreciate it but neither is it obtrusive. *Rocky* differs from most recent thrillers, for instance, in that its pace is written into the script, not decided later at the Steenbeck. The direction by John Avildsen (who directed *Joe* and *Save the Tiger* as well as many turkeys) is for the most part restrained. The cinematography is by John Crabe but could easily be by Haskell Wexler. The visual style is one of urban believability; the resulting texture is one too grainy for advertising, too glossy for real life. No one will find any fault with those people or with Stallone as an actor, who brings new life to familiar situations without betraying custom. The fault rather is with Stallone as a writer. His stereotypes, frankly, are inconsistent. About an hour and a half into the film, he decides to make a different type of movie than the one he started out doing.

Many commentators have compared *Rocky* with Paddy Chayefsky's *Marty*, a comparison I find inadequate at best. Marty, as played by Ernest Borgnine, was a loser because he was sunk in a mental and emotional state that afforded no challenges or even decisions. He was a moral and aesthetic vegetable. The only tension in the film came in his having to decide whether he wished to remain one. He was a figure, not beneath contempt, but beyond all consideration, since he simply refused to accept responsibility for his life. Rocky is much different. He's in control of his emotions and his being. He's a gentle fellow, tolerant of others, kind to animals. When a decision is called for (about whether to break a

76

debtor's thumbs as instructed) he takes the side of compassion. If he has a problem, it is that he's made peace with the establishment, or that part of it accessible to the derelict blue-collar society of Philadelphia. When the proprietor of the local gymnasium (Burgess Meredith, who has recently gone from character actor to freak impersonator) accuses him of selling out his athletic talent to work for gangsters, Rocky responds with a silence that is neither agreement nor rebuttal. The question is not whether he's sold out but whether he has invested wisely, trading lower-class comforts for a chance to rise above them materially.

The story also concerns Rocky's attempt to win the heart of a mousy pet shop clerk, played by Talia Shire, who in real life is Francis Ford Coppola's sister. He is encouraged in the pursuit by her brother, a meatcutter of alcoholic disposition. All this is beautifully realised though it leaves one to wonder where the film is headed. The answer is: downhill.

In a concurrent plot the audience is not aware of until later, the reigning heavyweight champion is promoting a multi-million dollar fight to be held in Philadelphia on the occasion of the American Bicentennial. The champion, who is modelled shamefacedly on Muhammad Ali and portrayed by Carl Weathers the former footballer, suffers a setback in his plans when his opponent fractures his hand during training. Aware that the bout is a media event not a true test of skill, he decides to fight an unknown Italian-American, a true son of Columbus. He chooses Stallone. The intrusion of all this hokum (as distinct from honest stereotyping) changes the entire mood and course of the film. From this point on, *Rocky* is predictability compounded by slickness.

Now that he has a shot at the title, Rocky is buttered up by all those who once rebuked him. He does not, however, unlike the film itself, go Hollywood. He trains hard and alone, knowing that he can never win. He wants only to go the full fifteen rounds to redeem himself not so much in his own eyes as in those of the people who convinced him of his inadequacy. He has known all along that he was their equal as a human being — a kindly, together fellow no more heir to careerism than the rest of us. Now he has been put in the ludicrous position of having to better himself in commercial terms so that, later, as a has-been, he might be seen as their peer.

Hereafter the story ceases to be that of the main character who has been so skillfully and simply developed. Instead we are

77

bombarded with glittery Hollywood clichés. The Ali figure (who is about as subtle a representation as the similar character in Russ Meyer's *Beyond the Valley of the Dolls*) is shocked when Rocky does not acquiesce to his punches but gives as good as he receives. Meredith, who serves as Rocky's manager, replays vicariously the glory of his own youth. The meatcutter, seeing that Rocky might yet win the decision, rejoices at the prospect of having so famous a common law brother-in-law. And the girlfriend, who averts her eyes from the scenes of blood, rushes into the ring afterward. As she does so, Rocky, bruised and banged up and in defeat, turns his back to the fans and the media and screams out his love for her. The film ends with a frozen frame of their embrace. The soundtrack finishes with the shouts of reunion and the din of glory mixed in one great piercing noise. Too bad.

A part of the comparison with *Marty*, it seems to me, is nothing more than the fact that Rocky has a very 1950s feel to it, in keeping with what, until the end, is the simple grace of the narrative. In a way, the feel is sustained by the direction even after the story loses sight of its original purpose. One comes away, for instance, with the impression that *Rocky* has been a violent film. In fact, there is no physical violence of the kind we are used to even in films not known for their brutality. Even the long fight scenes show little blood. It is merely that Stallone, although depicting a gentle character, gives the impression of repressed violence. Similarly, one might recall the film as having been rough in its language. Actually, though, it contains not one four letter word. The suggestion of profanity is created by the boxers trying to speak through their protective mouthpieces, as if muttering under their breath.

Such aspects are skillfully handled. It is difficult to avoid the conclusion, however, that a two-hour film has been made of a one-hour idea. Once the character development reaches an impasse, Stallone opts for Hollywood, taking the others along with him. Until the introduction of Weathers and his new plot, the pace of the film is eccentrically rhythmical. Afterwards, there are many short, tight scenes to heighten our emotional ties to the character of Rocky once the script no longer justifies such sympathy. Even the musical score, by Bill Conti, which before was so casual and effective, becomes at the end a Hollywood sellout, using everything short of bagpipes to arouse our emotions. *Rocky*, sorry to say, comes to a bad end.

April 1977

III

Although it would be presumptuous to do so, one might be tempted to try getting a sense of *Islands in the Stream*, the film adaptation of Hemingway's posthumously published novel, just by running down the credits. Its stars George C. Scott. Therefore it is not likely to seem as though anyone else of equal rank is in the cast. The director is Franklin J. Schaffner, who made *Patton, Papillon* and *Nicholas and Alexandra* — movies that were epics or wished to be. The fact that the cinematographer, Fred Koenekamp, also shot *Towering Inferno*, and that the writer, Denne Bart Petitclerc, comes directly from television, could also carry weight. Judging from these facts, one could easily expect *Islands in the Stream* to be a big film, with tall acting, exotic locations, powerful scenes and plenty of primary colours. A big film and probably a ragged one for all its mechanical ease.

As it happens, *Islands in the Stream* does in fact have all those elements. It delivers the stuff of which Hemingway's reputation was made outside the literary world and for which his books were read, superficially, by a pulp audience with cultural pretensions. But it is not a gutsy film, nor a particularly serious one. The novel published in 1970 was the edited version of a sprawling manuscript that Hemingway had been working on intermittently for decades and which he had already looted for *The Old Man and the Sea*. The present movie, while not a strict translation for the screen, is not altogether a job of butchering either. It is true to the spirit of Hemingway's personality as it has come down to us through memoirs, biographies, self-promotions and earlier films. It will satisfy those who for various reasons have not read either Cole's notes or the real thing.

The mere idea of a film enshrining or capitalising on a famous novelist's book is itself pretty old-fashioned. It reeks of the 1930s and 1940s when the big studios were vying for material with which to assuage their crassness while at the same time turn a buck. Film, frankly, has gone beyond being a sort of Book-of-the-Month Club. I daresay both film and fiction are better for such growth.

Although the film includes the texture and sound of the novel (and also, in one scene, some ridiculously stilted dialogue), it diverges widely from the book. In the novel, Thomas Hudson, a sculptor living in the Bahamas in 1940, is visited by his three sons. Later his

79

former spouse arrives to tell him that she is remarrying and that one of the sons has been killed in the war. Later still, and for complicated reasons, Hudson also goes to war, chasing German submarines in his fishing boat. In the end, if memory serves, he survives. But in the film he knows telepathically that his son is dead, making redundant the visit by his ex-wife, played by Claire Bloom. More importantly, Scott-as-Hudson, instead of entering the war, sets out for the States. On the way, he is killed while helping smuggle Jewish refugees into Cuba.

In the old days of Hollywood, novels were restructured in that way for commercial reasons, to create better box office for the stars who were eating up the profits or to appease a huge audience on whom psychology was lost. Here, though, one has the sense that changes were made to satisfy our conception of Hemingway the person and performer. Thomas Hudson was, of course, perhaps even more than Nick Adams or Jake Barnes, Hemingway's idea of himself. Scott's Hudson is thoroughly (but not self-consciously) *our* conception of Hemingway's view of himself. As a consequence, the role appears deeper than it is. The cinematic Hudson is a cold and one-dimensional fellow for all his paternal love and his brooding. Scott, knowing this weakness in the script, has sought to make it seem only a defect of the man he portrays, thereby heightening the Hemingwayness of it all. Wisely, he stops short of the alternative of dominating every scene. My tentative opinion is that this, with those in *The Last Run* and *Rage*, could be remembered as his choicest roles — far better than *Patton*, which was merely the flashiest.

Islands in the Stream is not an actor's film or a director's, it is entirely for the audience. People who have affection for Hemingway without knowing much about him would prefer to think of him (or his fictional *Doppelgänger*) dying in a burst of hostile gunfire, as in the film, not as he did in actuality. They are the people who subconsciously lump together Hemingway and Bogart. One of the stock elements of Bogart movies, as Peter Bogdanovich pointed out, was "the fellow who thought he took care [of Bogart], the rummy, the piano player, the one *he* took care of, the one you didn't mess with." Perhaps the best such role was Walter Brennan's in *To Have and Have Not*, one that was in this and other respects a Hollywood exaggeration. In the novel itself, the rummy character was minor; he became important in the film only because William Faulkner, as adapter, got carried away trying to concoct or restore some real Hemingway touches to the script. Unknowingly and probably uncaringly, Faulkner was helping weld Hemingway and Bogart together for generations to come. The result is that, in the film *Islands in the Stream*, the part of the puffy and derelict Englishman, played by David Hemmings, is much more important than in the novel.

That the movie is more a tribute to the public extra-literary idea of Hemingway than to the book itself is further shown by the fact that, at a time when Hemingway's artistic reputation has never been lower, films of his work have never been more numerous. Already being planned are a John Huston adaptation of *Across the River and Into the Trees* with Richard Burton and another version (the third) of *A Farewell to Arms*. It would seem, then, that like Fitzgerald, Hemingway is beginning to have a reputation based not on his works but on films catering to the general idea of the person who wrote them.

Through legend, memoirs and even television, the public has come to see Fitzgerald not as an artist but as the quintessential famous loser of recent times, as the poor son of a bitch for whom nothing, either professional or personal, went right. We have found it difficult to divorce this image from his works when going to see the films those books inspire. As a result, we come away from the recent films of *The Great Gatsby* and *The Last Tycoon* believing that the curse plagues him still, even in death. It is in one sense just as well that what are undoubtedly more satisfying scripts, such as Truman Capote's version of *Gatsby* or Christopher Isherwood's *The Beautiful and the Damned*, lie unproduced. A well made movie from a Fitzgerald book would bewilder an audience. We go to such movies expecting to be disappointed and come away satisfied at being let down.

Hemingway's case is not the same, though he too has a posthumous movie reputation. It is based, it seems to me, on the fact that his social ideas (as distinct from his artistic ones, which the films avoid) are now outdated. No one any longer mistakes grace under pressure for morality. Being a man in the macho sense runs counter to the fight against sexual inequality. Struggling against Nature seems passé at best now that we are attempting to conserve it. So we attend *Islands in the Stream* and the films to follow expecting to see an intellectual period piece. We want a faithful reproduction of what we half remember and perhaps misunderstand. That is why *Islands in the Stream* works. It's a better movie than half of the credits imply. It is also a less energetic and imaginative film than the other half would suggest.

May 1977

IV

Each of the ten James Bond films to date has ended with an announcement of the one to follow. Thus the last movie, *The Man with the Golden Gun*, in 1974, closed with a blurb forewarning us of *The Spy Who Loved Me*. Now in turn, *The Spy Who Loved Me* concludes with a reference to *For Your Eyes Only*, which doubtless will follow in a couple of years. Clearly, the time is not far distant when the producers of the series will have run out of Ian Fleming originals. This eventuality, however, is not likely to stop them, for already they are working without benefit of text. *The Spy Who Loved Me* not only has little in common with the book of the same title, much of its tone and flavour, inevitably, runs counter to that of the books and the other films before it.

Fleming, a man of despicable instincts, was writing at a time when the Cold War showed no signs of warming into today's wary and mutually distrustful cordiality. He was trafficking in people's ignorance of one another as well as their apprehension. Also, he was working when patriotism had not yet given way to cynicism, though people were even then conceding that diplomacy often entailed a certain cruelty and underhandedness. Not only Fleming but far more substantial writers, such as John Le Carré and Len

Deighton, were giving the public its first real taste of what they believed were the actual innerworkings of modern espionage, the continuation of war by political means. Today all this appears ludicrous, old fashioned, wrongheaded and silly. That it could ever have seemed otherwise is a source of amazement.

There are many reasons why now it is difficult to take Bond seriously, and in the present film the producers have tried to meet each objection. For one thing, the whole profession has at last fallen into deserved disrepute. At a time when we know that the CIA has overturned foreign governments, hounded its fellow citizens, put mafiosi on the payroll, used torture and poison, repeatedly tried to kill Fidel Castro and, we suspect, had some hand in political assassinations inside its own country — at such a time it is hard to see any glamour in Bond. The fact that he is English, not American, only makes him more incredible now than when he began: twenty years ago it was still possible for some to believe Britain was a sort of world power.

It was necessary therefore in this film to show Bond as part of an international rather than merely British team, working for the safety of the world, not just the western bloc. Thus we have a plot in which the British and the Russians join forces to foil a private individual rather than some other government — in this case, a fellow who captures British and Russian nuclear submarines and wants to devastate the earth. The plot, as I say, was worked out by the writers, Christopher Wood and Richard Maibaum. Wisely, they omitted the character of Felix Leiter, the CIA operative who in past films has sometimes joined in the excitement. Leiter would be laughed and hooted off the screen even by the natural constituents of this series.

The heroes, then, have changed and so have the villains. The essentially bigoted nature of Fleming's originals were long adhered to on the screen. His bad guys in the past were Dr No (a known oriental) and Blofeld and Goldfinger (whom we were not left to doubt were Jews). Today it is getting more difficult for racists to get away with such stereotypes. Recent nemeses (Christopher Lee last time, now Curt Jurgens) are not even Third World types, much less inscrutable or avaricious. Whatever this shift has done to soothe the producers' collective conscience, it has mitigated still further the spirit of Fleming, who was essentially reactionary, xenophobic and anti-Semitic in his approaches to problems, real and fictional. There are also interesting changes (or lack of changes)

in the other basic components of the books and previous films —
the girls and gadgets.

As difficult as it is to imagine today, *Dr No*, in 1962, and *From
Russia With Love*, the following year, were in their time considered
risqué and even dirty. Now they seem far less raunchy than the
ads in the underground. That Fleming held women in low esteem
is a commonplace. So is the theory that he wrote of them as he did
to compensate for his shyness and bumbling in real life (his former
secretary at the *Sunday Times*, who lives in Toronto, once told me
that he used to blush whenever another woman entered his office).
Now Bond's women are just beginning to change.

Barbara Bach, who plays Major Anya Amasova of the Red Army,
the collaborator of Bond (Roger Moore), is squarely within the
Fleming mould. She has that pouting expressing and a cantilever
body; she's strong-willed enough to be challenging but never so
agile and clever as Bond himself, for whom she inevitably takes a
spill. But the fact that she is this time of equal rank and does not
take off her clothes quite so promiscuously as her predecessors
may, just may, count for something, I'm not sure.

The gadgetry too is interesting but for the opposite reason. It has
all but stood still as other aspects of the films have been altered.
Reality was always running closely behind these devices and now
seems to have overtaken them. All the films tend to run together
in one's memory but it was, I believe, in *Goldfinger*, cinematically
the most intriguing of the lot, that Bond was bound supine to a
table as a laser was threatening to render him into two equal parts.
The device used in the book, if I'm not mistaken, was a simple buzz
saw. Working with a property even then a few years old, the
filmmakers were forced to come up with something a bit more fan-
tastic.

Here their imaginations seem to have failed them as technology
has made most of their old tricks clichés. The principal gadgets in
this film seem to be a parachute (a parachute for God's sake!
Leonardo!) and an automobile fitted with machine guns and a
smokescreen (similar to that used in one of the old Sean Connery
films). True, this new improved model does convert to a mini-
submarine but in doing so only brings to mind the underwater
scooters in *Thunderball*. Like his cinematic executors, Fleming was
less concerned with science and technology than pop trivia — was
less a former intelligence man with political savvy than a *Sunday
Times* editor with a superficial interest in trends — and his decades-

old enthusiasms have worn badly.

But then so has the whole concept. It stems, after all, from a period when we still thought it possible for one person to save us all. Now we question the very plausibility of being saved. Taken as trash and considered in light of society, the Bond pictures have been superseded by the kung fu ones, whose violence is open-handed not closemouthed, in which the Third World gets back its own and the female actors do much kicking of the male ones in the groin. Even Bond's violence is corny. I got no sense of this until, weeks after seeing the film itself, I happened upon the trailer for it. Of sex and cleverness this had little. Instead it was edited to show a long series of car crashes. It resembled nothing so much as one of those American-International pictures with Burt Reynolds as the good ole boy moonshiner outwitting the smokeys in the backwoods of Georgia. James Bond, who once seemed appropriate to the tonier Odeons, has fallen to the level of the drive-ins.

September 1977

V

Studios in the 1930s and 1940s had mottos such as "More stars than there are in heaven" and "It it's a Metro picture, it's the best show in town this week." The point, rather hard to grasp today, is that these organisations maintained large stock companies, ground out pictures in a matter of weeks and (since they owned their own theatre chains) changed the bills very frequently indeed. Their money went into general overhead, not usually into individual film properties; and such movies as *Casablanca* and *The Big Sleep* were lucky accidents. The result was the genre picture. Dick Richards shares the common affection for these old films and keeps trying to duplicate their style and texture without much success, as he tries now with *March or Die*, a Foreign Legion epic. All the standard elements are lovingly recreated: the brutal commanding officer (Gene Hackman), the angelic young recruit (Terence Hill), the woman with a past (Catherine Deneuve), the Arab tribesmen who look suspiciously Anglo-Saxon, the bloodless battle scenes and the sand. But the mood is gone. The essence of genre movies derives from their having been made quickly and cheaply in black-and-white. Ideally they were shot from scripts written by people who had sold one novel to Liveright in '28 and directed by some ginsodden hand who otherwise passed his time in Musso Frank's. Spending years to make one, panchromatically and on location, for $9.5 million, just doesn't work. *March or Die* was produced by Sir Lew Grade, who is known affectionately in Wardour Street as Sir Lew Greed.

December 1977 – January 1978

VI

On the surface, *Star Wars* by George Lucas owes its astounding popularity to its blend of slickness and its reverence for science fiction clichés. My own feeling, though, is that a large part of its appeal is the way it incorporates elements from many other sorts of film as well. It has, for instance, a tin woodsman except that he is now a robot, apparently gay, whose armour is gold lamé. Similarly, there is a lot of stuff from wartime American and British propaganda movies: bandits at four o'clock, and so on. Carrie Fisher (the daughter of Eddie) as the imperilled heroine affects the hairstyle and costume of Aimee Semple Macpherson without, like Jean Simmons in *Elmer Gantry*, actually resorting to Four Square Baptist dogma. It is said that the final scene is a frame-by-frame borrowing from Leni Riefenstahl's *Triumph of the Will*, though I have yet to compare them. Seeing *Star Wars* saves one from looking again at a number of old films in their entirety. A sort of *That's Entertainment 2001*.

December 1977 – January 1978

VII

Towards the beginning of Norman Jewison's otherwise inept 1969 film *Gaily Gaily* there's a technically stunning scene in which Jewison pulls back and back and back, revealing Chicago's Loop as it was in 1910, agag with traction cars and huddled masses in cloth caps. Few of the period buildings remain standing in the Loop itself, so Jewison shot the scene in Milwaukee, mocking up where necessary with plywood and papier mâché. This is precisely the sort of scene he does so well for he has a way with visual facts (Thomas Crown's house, Rod Steiger's sheriff's office). Not only does he pick the right set directors but the manner in which he uses their work to brief us on the lives of his people is neither blatant nor distracting nor too slick. One could say that Jewison's visual facts are often better handled than the characters. Jewison, let us not forget, is an old CBC man. At its most typical, his work is exactly what you would expect from a CBC man with unexpected millions in his budget.

His most recent film, *F.I.S.T.*, is similar to *Gaily Gaily*. It has one impressive historical recreation. This comes, in Cleveland in 1937, when striking teamsters, aided by the mob, trap the management goons and begin beating clubs on the paving bricks before closing in for the kill. But the remainder of the film never matches, in human and imaginative terms, the newsreel immediacy of this one scene. Instead it limps along blandly, taking its power from the fact that it's a *film à clef*.

Sylvester Stallone, who insists on writing roles for himself, plays Johnny Kovack (read Jimmy Hoffa). In order to make powerful the Federation of Interstate Truckers (read Teamsters), he accepts the help of the syndicate, against the advice of his colleague Abe Belkin (read Harold Gibbons, the union's longtime vice-president). This seals his doom, as years later a Senate rackets investigator named Andrew Madison (that is, Rod Steiger as Robert Kennedy) nails him for this indiscretion of youth. Kovack is about to testify against the mob, ridding himself of both the stigma and the actual presence, when he's gunned down in his home.

It's foolish to pretend that *F.I.S.T.* is any less a piece of keyhole gossip than, for example, *The Greek Tycoon*. The fact that the film is not really fiction, however, makes more and not less important the way it approaches the material. In this regard Jewison shows his faults. He deliberately avoids any concept which might be difficult to convey. Thus a scene showing the negotiation of a collective agreement, a process that's central to labour but not exactly cinematic, is made laughably simplistic, while a blowup in a Senate committee room, which is a meaningless play for media attention by all concerned, is handled with some care.

More basic is his determination to avoid politics. The Belkin character, for example, doesn't seem to have ever been a socialist, like the real-life Gibbons. And the central crisis in the movie is a moral one involving Kovack and the mob whereas a more honest film would have it otherwise. Hoffa was greedy but he was no more a gangster than he was an innocent dupe of gangsters. What he was most decidedly was a foe to Bobby Kennedy, a ruthless and dangerous demagogue who, had he ever gained the presidency, would likely have taken the abuse of power for personal reasons to heights not dreamed of by Richard Nixon. *F.I.S.T.*, however, pays lip service to the official myths concerning both Kennedy and the mob.

In doing so, it ignores the real story of American labour: the shift from left to right. To have shown that the movement was ever leftwing would have offended its members, the present audience. And to have shown them as rightwing would have infringed on their belief in a romanticised, sanitised past. Far be it from Jewison to shatter any myths. In fact, he shot two endings for this film, one in which Kovack survives the mob the triggermen, one in which he does not. He then showed both to preview audiences and circulated cards asking them to state their preference. We chuckled when the compositor pulled Orson Welles' two page-one proofs, KANE ELECTED and FRAUD AT POLLS. But this is different. This is important to reality, not just to the development of a character. Jewison's behaviour in this film has not been that of a director who takes his moral and artistic responsibility as seriously as his technique.

October – November 1978

Recent Westerns

The trick to being a moralist is to be consistent. It is perhaps a lack of consistency, as well as a move towards historical sophistication, that best distinguishes the current crop of westerns. The first feature ever made in Hollywood was a western and the last one could well be a western too. Westerns aren't really about the west but about the ethical preoccupations of the time in which they're made. That is why the genre has never become totally respectable and never gone completely out of fashion: it's always useful for putting forward one's present contradictions, if not for resolving them. In this context it is interesting that Robert Altman, Arthur Penn and Don Siegel have all turned to westerns recently. They are not directors normally associated with the form, the first two known for style over subject, and the third for his urban crime movies such as *Madigan*.

Altman, whose film is *Buffalo Bill and the Indians, or Sitting Bull's History Lesson*, is perhaps the least likely to have made such a film and the most natural one to have made it into something distinctly his own. With Altman the content is almost nothing and the manner everything. His style is elliptical and loose, yet full of little goodies. He knows only one technique — making a tightly structured film seem unstructured to avoid accusations of slickness. He has only one trick — cramming in lines and images that even drive-in audiences can perceive as adding up to something resembling a moral point of view. His equivalent in music is Robbie Robertson and the Band during the middle period. In literature it is Thomas Beer and Beer's successor E.L. Doctorow (who has a bit part in *Buffalo Bill* and whose novel *Ragtime* Altman is filming next).

Buffalo Bill is the most modern of all the films in its view of history. Most early westerns were merely stories set in the past in which good men triumphed over evil men. Only later did the notion evolve that everyone has a bit of both and the one with the more good wins. Constant self-doubt and Christian wishy-washiness created in some filmmakers a tension that elevated such a view to another level. John Ford, for instance, at his most characteristic, was but the second unit director of an inscrutable God looking over his shoulder, though two other facts helped make Ford distinctive. One was that he was a landscape moralist who made Nature his personal icon: the other was that he felt a sincere sense of loss at the subdivision of the wide open spaces and the end of a way of life. That was something that is now incorporated into westerns only as part of the premise, like the cowboy's relationship with the schoolmarm or the strife between cattlemen and sheepmen. Altman is modern by comparison in that he cannot even remotely conceive of a society not thoroughly urban. As for Nature, he rightly looks upon the Rockies as kitsch.

Altman does more to report the spirit of the times than to impose upon it. Like *M*A*S*H* and to a lesser extent *Nashville, Buffalo Bill* is black humour — but not too black and not very humorous. It takes the view of history that fools and losers underlie the figures in textbooks. In this case, textbook history is represented by William Cody, the one-time hunter and Custer scout who, by becoming Buffalo Bill and creating the wild west show, bridged the gap into modern times.

One cannot say there is actually a story here, for Altman's films are usually long loops of activity, chunks rather than slices of life. Basically, though, the film concerns Cody (Paul Newman) as a conniving clod in league with venal businessmen to profit from an idealised west which the cinematograph, an invention just around the corner, would mythologise ever more. The only other dimension comes with the introduction of Sitting Bull (Frank Kaquits) and his Sioux companion (Will Sampson) who match if not best him at his own game while managing to remain true to their past and conscious of their even more unpleasant future.

Cody is a phoney but a true phoney, aware as his patrons are that what he's serving up is comedic melodrama. His Custer-length hair turns out to be a wig. His marksmanship with a pistol is shown to be a cheap trick. He's even revealed as a failure in bed. The Sioux meanwhile are held up as logical, honest, low key and more than a little humourless. The contrast is more a proof of Gresham's law than a revisionist view of race relations.

It all must seem terribly fresh and even a bit shocking, in a giggly sort of way, to those who insist they can watch Altman films time and again and each time find something new. The truth, however, is that Altman keeps mistaking content for meaning. His style is to please both those who enjoy Hollywood slickness and those who don't. His films appear formless. They roll out never-endingly, like loo paper (a metaphor that needn't go any further). All the while, they are tight with the kind of overlapping dialogue that Howard Hawks picked up from Ben Hecht about thirty-five years ago. In Altman films everyone talks harshly and at once, like a congregation of deaf taxi despatchers. It's all a wonderful cartoon.

The more intriguing aspect of *Buffalo Bill* is Altman's use of history. In his casual way he manages to pin down a certain small truth about westerns and the time they supposedly depict. He gives a good demonstration of the salient fact that westerns, after all, deal with the Victorian era and, what's more, the Victorian era in a vaguely frontier society in which people tried to over-compensate for their crudity. The film is full of bad art objects of the type we chuckle over in antique stores. It virtually reeks of overstuffed furniture and overfed humans, including Pat McCormick as President Grover Cleveland. Everything has too much fringe on it or too many bangles or else contains too many long sentences. Altman used this veneer of authenticity to show the evolution of the western myth.

Also appearing in *Buffalo Bill* are Burt Lancaster and Joel Grey. The former plays Ned Buntline, the nineteenth-century pulp writer who created many of the farfetched frontier stereotypes Hollywood would later embrace with such alacrity. Sensing that he has created a monster, he says to Cody, sardonically, "It was the thrill of my life to have invented you." The other character, played by Grey, is Cody's manager, and he speaks the way a *Variety* deskman writes. Cody, he states, "is the most futurable act in our history." He later avows his intention to "Codify the world." These sound like recent coinages from the J. Walter Thompson agency but they probably aren't. After all, Mark Twain was forever using such verbs as "filthify," meaning to make vulgar.

Thus Altman points up the natural link between past commercialism and the effect of our own popular culture on future history. He conveys the idea that going into wild west shows was simply what people like Sitting Bull (or Gabriel Dumont for that matter) did once they outlived their power. Dressing up for Victorian ladies was what famous miscreants, safe but poor and without prospects, did to get by. It is perhaps a statement on both show business and art that in our time the popular villains, like some of the popular heroes, have taken to writing bad novels instead.

In Altman's film there is really only this one idea, which he beats to death with a stick. The shaded area between frontier and cityscape is also the locale of Arthur Penn's *The Missouri Breaks*. Here, by contrast, the historical idea dies of strangulation after putting up a good fight against a kind of inconsistency so uncertain that it spills over into the feel and flow of the end product.

The Missouri Breaks, which brings together Marlon Brando and Jack Nicholson for the first time, was written by Thomas McGuane, who is practically the only serious American novelist of the present time to have accomplished something as a director (namely, *Rancho De Luxe* and *92 in the Shade*). This is the first screenplay he has written not based on one of his own books and not directed by him. Since Penn has never been, like Hitchcock, a writer's director, this situation leads to rivalry. The rivalry in turn becomes confusion. There are grating visual non sequiturs, such as sudden wardrobe changes for no apparent reason, and annoying textual slip-ups, when Brando alters his name, identity, and accent without obvious underlying cause. Beneath all that, however, is enough harmony between script and direction on the one hand and performance on the other to make the theme work and even to provide one or two important scenes.

The setting is Montana ("the breaks of the Missouri River") in the 1880s, a period when such backwaters were rapidly being filled in by cartographers. Brando, by all indications a bounty hunter, stands for the frontier and the past. He has lived his life outdoors to the extent that he now feels most comfortable when dwarfed by the massive stature of the countryside. While he is easily adaptable to the new urban civilisation that is springing upon him, he is also resentful of it. The resentment gets directed towards Nicholson, a younger fellow who lives on the geographical and chronological cusp between wilderness and city and who, given a choice, would prefer the latter. Nicholson has no say, however, at least in the matter of his age, and so finds that his own moral deterioration is keeping pace with the receding of the forest. When we see him he's living a double life. Part of him is the rancher he really wants to be, waiting for the countryside around him to be built up. Part is the reluctant rustler trying to make ends meet. Brando sees through the first part of this split personality to the second and makes it his target.

Such conflict reaches a climax in the most important and most thoroughly realised scene of the film. Brando and Nicholson have been chasing each other all day around what remains of the unfenced countryside. Brando thinks he can easily defeat Nicholson, a mere parvenu and weakling. Nicholson believes just the opposite, that the advantage rests with him as the younger man more in step with the times. Exhausted, they both bed down for the night some miles apart.

Here we see Brando at his best, in one of those scenes (like Godfather Corleone playing with his grandson) that makes a historical type real. Brando's horse, tethered to a picket rope, refuses to go to sleep quickly, the way horses will. Certain that no one's watching but a bit self-conscious just the same, Brando takes out his harmonica and plays the animal a little tune. He speaks nonsense in the horse's ear, using what in the dubbed French version must surely be the familiar *tu* form. He then stretches out on the ground and falls asleep himself.

For a brief moment, Penn uses the camera-eye technique (in which the lens sees only and exactly what Brando sees), a technique everyone has been afraid to use since Robert Montgomery nearly ruined it for all time with his 1946 film *Lady in the Lake*. For a moment we see only the sky, as Brando sees it lying on his back midway between consciousness and unconsciousness. Then slowly the screen fades to black as Brando lapses into sleep. Time passes: it could be five minutes or five hours. Brando hears an odd noise and wakes with a jolt to see Nicholson's grimy face inches away from his own. "The noise you heard," Nicholson is saying softly, "was me cutting your throat." We do not see the gore. We see only the disbelief in Brando's eyes, as if to say *This can't be happening to me! This isn't right! I'm supposed to win!* It's the expression Nixon wore as he boarded the helicopter the last time for San Clemente and infamy.

It is a fine scene but only in the context of the whole, which is as it should be. It shows the final score as civilisation — one and frontier — nought; and as this is part of an American film, one is not necessarily pleased with such an outcome. Like many other recent U.S. westerns (from say, *The Wild Bunch* onwards but distinct from the so-called spaghetti westerns) it adds another dimension to the symbolism of advancing metropolis, receding frontier. It uses youth to signify the former and middle and old age the latter. That is something done much better, if perhaps less subtly, in *The Shootist*, a film that would be easy to avoid seeing if one were to base the decision solely on the credits and the advertisements.

Here, in Don Siegel's film, a vehicle for John Wayne, all the small details of time and place are filled in. It is 1901 and Carson City, Nevada, once a tough mining town, has telephones, dry cleaners, a few horseless carriages, a network of streetcars, soon to be electrified. It is into such a setting that Wayne, a gunfighter who created a disturbance there almost a generation earlier, comes to await his death. It sounds like a premise that could go either way. Despite a few coy scenes, it reaches a level of psychological intensity uncommon in Hollywood films if not unprecedented in westerns. Wayne seems to grow into the role of the vicious old son of a bitch who, ironically, is dying of cancer now that he is beginning to mellow. Even better is the sense of human continuity unbroken by death.

Word of Wayne's presence and ailment soon leaks and everyone tries to take advantage of him. The creepy old undertaker (John Carradine) wants to make money exhibiting his corpse. A callous newspaperman wants to cash in by writing a totally erroneous pulp biography. Even the local barber plans to sell the tufts of the gunfighter's hair he has swept up from the floor, along with those of his other customers.

This is the most demanding part of Wayne's career. For once his acting or non-acting coincides almost exactly with the characterisation before him. It's not that Wayne the actor and the personality represents in our day the nineteenth-century man (his politics, for instance, may be eighteenth century). Nor is it merely that Wayne in real life has survived what he's wont to call the Big C. It's rather that the hesitant bedraggled style of his, a sort of enervated bravado, is perfect in this context. For years impressionists have made a career of Wayne's distinctive walk while ignoring his most characteristic gesture and attitude, which involves a sigh, raised eyebrows and a sudden decision to change expression. It is the gesture of a tired old man deciding whether he still has the energy or indeed still cares to have it. It is essential to the character he portrays in *The Shootist*. It is also germane to a character who represents society entering upon a new century. It seems to indicate a failure to find much worth saving in the past he is nonetheless rooted in and attached to. It seems to sigh in the face of an uncertain future. All of this fits in nicely with and even summarises the attitude Siegel and his screenwriters, Miles Hood Swarthout and Scott Hale, are taking towards the past.

Usually it has been only in saloon scenes that American westerns have given any indication of the cheap opulence of Victorian life. Elsewhere they have depended too much on streets lined with wooden false-front buildings which, despite their exposure to the elements, never show signs of wear. It is as though all the locations are one amorphous boom town, erected all at once in a never-never land where the boom always lingers, never falters or swells, and everything stays the same. That was the view at mid-century, as exhibited for example in all those cheap Audie Murphy films of the 1950s and early 1960s. That westerns are beginning to change all that is a sign of our uncertainty now that the twenty-first century is creeping up on us.

The Shootist reflects such changes quite well, though with varying degrees of subtlety and finesse. It is a bit too simple, for instance, when, riding into town at first, Wayne buys a newspaper to learn that Queen Victoria has died. It is also a bit much when, seeking to capture the feel of nineteenth-century speech, the script sidesteps the authentic rhetoric of *True Grit* in favour of rewritten clichés. By this method, the old cowboy line "Gee, you're pretty when you're mad" becomes "You have a fine colour when you're on the sore." What the film does do, however, is to create a feeling of authenticity through the set direction by Arthur Parker. Here is the saloon interior to end all saloon interiors: the real goods from a gaudy age one can still find traces of in some of the now rundown eastern hotels. Here too (in Lauren Bacall's boarding house, to which Wayne is sent by Jimmy Stewart, the doctor) is the perfect example of a Victorian household. The parlour has all the right pretensions, the kitchen all the proper utensils.

Such conscientiousness does not restore history but it does raise the troublesome question of film's relationship with the past. When Siegel, at the start of *The Shootist*, includes a montage of old John Wayne clips by way of flashing back to his protagonist's younger days, the effect is twofold. It illustrates the difference between the old style western and the new, for the Wayne shown in the old footage seems a very phoney character, with too much tailoring and too many modern mannerisms. And it raises the fact that history therefore is only our perception of it. That these clips nonetheless look more historical simply because technology has made them seem old. That perhaps it is no longer possible to convey history convincingly in other than black-and-white. And what it *is* possible to convey is not history but the opposite of history — continuity and sameness, what nineteenth-century poets with straight faces called the eternal verities.

At least Brando in *The Missouri Breaks* and, to a lesser extent, Wayne in *The Shootist*, succeed for a brief moment in showing that the way people now dead might have behaved under stress is not so different from the way we believe ourselves to behave. The rest is beyond our grasp, and no amount of period touches will be anything but so much research. It is behind this question of research — either too little at the expense of accuracy, or too much at the sacrifice of truth — that the western has always dwelt. Despite recent advances, it probably always will.

October 1976

Careers on the Wing

I

A certain sadness infects the viewer
after Orson Welles' new film *F for
Fake*. It hits him in that brief moment
when the screen is suddenly white
again, before he leaves his seat for the
lobby. It follows him out into the day-
light. It's a difficult feeling to pin
down and an easy one to mislabel. It
is not, I think now, a sadness in finding Welles' old style archaic and his
new one derivative. This film is a
documentary, a form Welles has
come to late in life, but it's fresh by
virtue of being vastly more selfindul-
gent than even the most innovative
NFB short. It's a documentary that
isn't really about anything very much
except its author's view of himself.

Nor is the feeling a realisation that
Welles himself is past his prime. He
has always been as important for
what he represents as for what he
does, so his career has no centre, only
a beginning. The sensation probably
arises from a shame and even anger
at what society has always done to the

few Orson Welleses of this planet — reduced them to buskers dancing on the pavement, hoping to be thrown a few coppers. Yes, this is what the sadness is all about. This is also what Welles would like us to believe is the subject of this film. *F for Fake* is about charlatans and Welles (he admits it) is one of them. At least it's his pretending to be a sharper which has made him one of the last and greatest of our artistic tricksters.

It has never been sufficiently recognised how deeply rooted Welles' personal style is in the 1890s. Like many other men of talent who came of age in the 1930s he looked back on the 1920s as a kind of belle epoque and on its bohemian artists as leaders of a great lost cause. That was normal enough. Welles, however, seems to have gone one step farther. He put himself in the psychic shoes of his 1920s forebears, who in turn had looked back fondly to what Thomas Beer christened the mauve decade. His attitude towards himself and his work — it is a sensibility bordering on an ethic — has always been that of an artist at war with society rather than merely alienated from it. This antiquated notion has a sort of period charm. In Welles, it seems to satisfy the natural historical bent to which bohemians are heir.

Welles has been, singly and sometimes all at once, a David Belasco type of character, who takes great delight in tricking his audience into mistaking what he does for art, and a sort of dayglo Augustus John: a big bull of an artist punctuating his anti-philistine rages with pretensions he considers his birthright as a genius. Perhaps the 1890s figure he most resembles is Frank Harris, who made a point of doing everything once — one decent novel, one remarkable biography, one play — just as Welles has done in film. His editing career, which began so brilliantly, ended in inevitable self-parody, just as Welles' acting career has done. The principal difference between them is that Welles has made modesty and self-depreciation as integral a part of his public personality as Harris made boisterousness and self-aggrandizement. Harris put his by-line ahead of his talent; Welles has drawn attention differently, by putting his own name last in the *Citizen Kane* credits. Harris proclaimed himself a great writer at the top of his lungs. Welles, wearing cloak and black fedora, shyly mumbles that he's a charlatan, a poseur, a mere conjurer in a roomful of healers. He loves it and the audience loves it. This film serves mainly to give Welles the opportunity of recreating his famous role, with more of the stops removed than customary.

99

The ostensible surface subject for *F for Fake* is Elmyr De Hory, the art forger. He was the subject of *Fake*, a biography by Clifford Irving, and is widely regarded for his Matisses, Picassos and especially his Modiglianis. We see him trotting around Ibiza, dashing off drawings and canvases by day, playing host to the island's expatriate community by night. But it's not quite so simple as this. There is a rapid series of escalating absurdities, with De Hory, whose spurious masters fool curators around the world, being interviewed by Irving, who was soon to be jailed for his bogus life of Howard Hughes. There is also an absolute dazzle of cross-cutting and mixes. The sham editing gets in the way of the hollowness of the performers discussing the transparency of their work. All this is heightened by much extraneous but momentarily convincing material — like false clues in a mystery story. And all that in turn, is several times stopped abruptly to allow Welles to reminisce about his own career.

He recalls his beginnings as an actor, when at sixteen he duped an Irish manager into believing he was already a Broadway star. He alludes to his work as a stage magician and mentions the Martian invasion broadcast of 1938. In one tantalizing bit of new information, which seeks to tie the film together but doesn't, it is revealed that *Citizen Kane* was based on Hearst only after the idea of basing a film on Howard Hughes had been discarded. Welles doesn't state this himself. Instead he wheels on Joseph Cotton to make the revelation. Cotton has greater credibility than Welles, who didn't even shoot the De Hory footage in the first place, but bought it. The question, of course, is whether Cotton is telling the truth and, even if he is, whether he's merely playing Jedediah Leland again to Welles' Charles Foster Kane.

If it had been made by anyone else, *F for Fake* would have been an infuriating film or a monotonous one. Made as it was by wily old Orson, it is, above all, a proud film, full of the self-mocking pride which comes in defeat through natural attrition and with which Welles seems to have been born. He's telling us that he is the last of the independents, hustling for pennies with which to make not films reflecting his art (those days are past, he implies with a sigh and a wink), but films revealing his artifice. He's doing well what Norman Mailer, for one, does badly. He's showing that he's an old warhorse worn down by the system but not regretting anything since it was all in the name of good fun and a good cause. Although blind with metaphorical cataracts, although surrounded by perfidious whelps and ridiculed (or lionized) at every corner, he still delivers the goods, to those who care. Such is the stance he assumes, part sad sack and part sagamore.

The difference between Welles and others who act this way is, of course, that with Welles the pose is at once a true assessment and a load of nonsense. No one has been harder on the system than Welles has, but no one has been harder on himself either. The truth about him lies somewhere between the hyperbole and reticence of his professional utterances. It is rarely revealed in his films. It is shown best, if shown at all, in the stories about him, of which there has never been a shortage. One such story, a revealing one, I believe, in light of *F for Fake*, runs something like this:

In the late 1940s, when Hearst was still doing his best to make him unemployable, Welles met the head of one of the quickie studios at a dinner party. Half in jest, the studio boss said that any script ideas Welles had would certainly be considered most carefully back at Monogram or Republic or wherever it was. Welles thereupon described in great detail a plot he said had been eating away at him for years. He went on at some length, acting out various of the parts. The boss was more impressed than anyone had ever seen him before. He and Welles drew up a tentative agreement at once.

The next morning, the studio chief called his subordinates together around the table, announcing that, for the usual meagre fee, the great young genius Orson Welles had agreed to do them an original. He related the intricate story just as Welles had told it to him. Then he sat back, waiting for chins to drop and appreciative palms to slap him on the back. Finally, at the back of the room, a weak voice was raised. "Herb," said the voice, "you've just bought *Macbeth*."

The same story could well be told about *F for Fake*, with the likes of David L. Wolper or some television network head substituted for the producer of B pictures. "David," the voice would say, "you've just bought *My Life and Loves*, only it's not the real one. It sounds as though it was written by Clifford Irving."

February 1976

101

II

Woody Allen's new film *Annie Hall* is such a synthesis of his other work — in fact of comedy's past and present strains — that it is practically a new form in itself. It is difficult to imagine him ever making a more balanced movie without ceasing to be the figure we know or without the audience undergoing a complete change. The latter would seem an almost more likely occurrence than the former. Allen has always been consistent. Indeed, consistency has been as much a source of woe as of glory. In Martin Ritt's *The Front*, for instance, he was supposed to be portraying a figure who was funny but too dumb to know why. But what he in fact played was the only character he knows — the one who's *bright* and funny. The film suffered badly as a result even though the audience, for the most part diehard Allen followers, still savoured the one-liners. That same audience, it follows naturally, should experience something like orgiastic delight at *Annie Hall*.

As writer and director of the film as well as star, Allen has achieved an ideal, though a deceptive one. It's true that most performers who have directed as well as starred in their own films have failed (Brando and George C. Scott, for instance). But it's equally true that those who've come nearest success have been the comedians, such as Fields and Mae West. Perhaps more than other types of performers, comedians are used to playing themselves, mechanically, and thus can bring the greater part of their attention to bear on actual filmmaking. In Allen's case, at least, this rule certainly holds true. *Annie Hall* is a skilfully made and at times cautiously experimental film, and Allen is playing himself to the extent that the whole exercise is titillatingly autobiographical.

His part is that of a comedian named Alvy Singer. Like Woody Allen, Singer was raised in Brooklyn and spent years writing for other comics before finding the perfect outlet for his own insecurities in appearing before small club and campus audiences and, later, in writing plays. Again like Singer, Allen was twice married, first to a stereotypical New York intellectual comer (played in the film by Janet Margolin) and later to Louise Lasser (here approximated by Carol Kane). But that is background. The movie is basically the story of Singer's relationship with Annie Hall, a WASP apprentice singer who has (to quote Richard Corliss) "the kind of sensual innocence that once inspired Botticelli and the Beach Boys."

This title role is undertaken by Diane Keaton, whom Allen once lived with and whose real name is Diane Hall (she probably changed it because it sounded too much like a dormitory). At any event, as well as being Allen's funniest film, it is also his most serious to date. It is sincere in trying to reconcile Singer's public life as a comedian with his private one as a decidedly tragic figure who wishes to be the dominant partner in any relationship but cannot abide anyone more passive than himself. In a sense then it is also intricately caught up in the singular relationship Allen has always enjoyed (and endured) with his audience.

Allen's career has been amazing in that while seldom even nodding in the direction of the lowest common denominator he has managed to please virtually everyone but the most congenitally humourless. He is in some measure, for instance, a slapstick artist; in *Annie Hall* he sets himself up for many visual gags (such as sneezing into $2,000 worth of cocaine) that will doubtless provoke guffaws in small children and municipal politicians. Then too he is like those other skilled comedic actors now popular, whose strength is their failure to deceive themselves. Allen is, all rolled into one, the equivalent of the characters played so often by Richard Benjamin (the unfailing ass), George Segal (the sophisticate who never quite makes it) and Elliott Gould (the loser who aspires to be hip). Every now and then he is even the old-fashioned jokester and spinner of stories.

Increasingly, though, and I think more importantly, he is the radical intellectual comedian, whose source of humour is an expensive education that has no other application. His largest and most appreciative audience are people in the same predicament — the ones whose parents borrowed on their life insurance to put them through school but who, nearing middle age, still don't know what they want to be. *Not only is there no God, but try getting a plumber on the weekend.* Anyone who can come up with that (to me, the quintessential Woody Allen line) is someone who has been through more than a casual brush with western philosophy. Someone, in fact, who is educated far beyond his ambition and so must joke about the fact. Jesting seems to him the only practical use to which his schooling can be put: a situation so absurd as to itself inspire a neverending cycle of black humour.

What makes this a radical stance is the fact that such people, the victims of parental trade union prosperity, are surely the great potential opposition. They have resisted under the cultural torture

103

of prime time television the demand that they confess their mediocrity. They have ended up (like the character Woody Allen portrays in his books, plays, films and most recently even comic strips) with nothing but a vocabulary and a few isolated scraps of ideas separating them from the vast, trackless suburbs where, in addition to a chicken in every pot, there are plaster flamingos on every lawn. His style caters to what the trades persist in calling the campus audience but which is actually made of those who've left the campuses — and stagnated because the universities have taught them little except how to propagate more individuals like themselves. In this milieu comedy is one of the principal forms of expression: in particular, a certain kind of post-standup comedy is overtly linguistic and of which Allen remains the best practitioner.

The question of who controls the language has lately done a complete turn-about that is quite interesting in this context. Only yesterday concern with the purity of English was limited to conservatives. Mostly they were teachers and linguistic amateurs. While such folks still abound (one thinks of Edwin Newman) they must face the fact that affection for language is increasingly the domain of radicals. It is no coincidence, for example, that the women's movement and the Quebec separatists — to name only two — have made moral issues of points of usage which before would have seemed out of place anywhere on the left. Custodianship of the language has become an important political consideration since it has come to be viewed as the necessary first step to control of the media. In entertainment the result has been a number of radical linguistic comedians such as George Carlin and Robert Klein (and to a lesser extent Richard Pryor and David Steinberg) who don't tell jokes so much as point out the absurdities in everyday language which reveal social absurdities.

Annie Hall fits nicely within that framework, with its jokes at the expense of William F. Buckley, its intimations of Hegel and Schopenhauer, its visual jokes in reference to certain Bergman films, and even one scene parodying *Goodbye, Columbus*. But if it delights in the proximity of a huge well-educated audience that couldn't have existed thirty years ago, it also veers away from part of what that audience has come to expect. The film plays down Singer's family, for instance, except to contrast it briefly with Annie's. The circumstances of growing up Jewish in New York have been dealt with to the extent that any further satire would seem a parody of earlier send-ups. And while there are many good one-liners and

104

gags, there are many that simply fail to work. I felt that some of them were included to reinforce the tacky world of failed jokes in which Singer lives. The point of Alvy Singer is that he is a natural clown who everywhere sees absurdity but that no one ever quite takes the clown's dilemma seriously, whatever its role in society. It is on this note, I'll wager, that Singer and the real Woody Allen become one. Conversely, the point of divergence is that Allen has used *Annie Hall* to analyse and maybe resolve the problem in a way Singer would never be capable of.

United Artists, in its ads, has been tagging the film "a romantic comedy about a contemporary urban neurotic." That, I believe, is fallacy. It is more a film about the impossibility of romantic comedy for someone who feels he belongs by rights elsewhere than in the modern middle class with which he has no sympathy — sort of the intellectual equivalent of the pre-op transsexual. Allen hasn't made the problem go away by making *Annie Hall*, of course. But by addressing it in such a way, using all the previously fragmented means at his disposal, he has at least examined it psychologically. His other films were usually clever ideas. Indeed some were ideas ahead of their time (in *What's Up Tiger Lily?* he was where Mel Brooks only now is with *Silent Movie*). At their best, however, they were only competent amusements stringing together gags and punchlines. But with *Annie Hall* he has brought his talent together for one purpose and in the process become something of an artist.

August 1977

III

Carl Reiner's work is insignificant in some rather important ways. A native of television, he's always tried branching out into other fields, with results that run from the competent to the amusing but never quite extend to the first rate. Television remains the source of his most cohesive and original work, yet the limitations of television are forever doing him in. He never quite succeeds in any other form for the same reasons he's always succeeded so well on the air. Saying all of this might seem a waste of time were not Reiner inextricably caught up in several currents of pop culture and were he not a kind of symbol for their poverty. He comes from that medium in which anyone who thinks a little bit seems to be a thoughtful person, in which anyone with several simple skills appears to be a polymath. Making the transition to the smaller, more sophisticated arena has exposed the shallowness of many such people; indeed, it's deprived many of the simple dignity of seeming to be *interesting*, much less brilliant. For every Woody Allen who's survived to find his rightful medium there are dozens of Steve Allens who are always in transit.

Reiner, of course, knows all this, for the television theme seems to have infiltrated every outside project he's ever undertaken. One finds TV dogma as well as TV technique, for example, in *Oh, God!* and *The One And Only*, the two feature films he's directed recently. But these elements can be traced back much further in his work. Specifically, back to the 1950s, television's salad days and also his own.

Comedy in those times still knew bounds, and testing them was part of the fun. Reiner was at his best as a writer and performer on Sid Caesar's *Your Show of Shows*, pieces of which stood up quite well when stitched together recently for theatrical release. With another comedy writer, Mel Brooks, he spun off the two-thousand-year-old man routine, which was popular for so long in clubs and on records. The idea was pure fifties: to disguise soft political humour as nonsatiric silliness through a premise that was run into the ground. As such, the concept was little different from that of *Oh, God!*, which one assumes Reiner had a big hand in writing, with Larry Gelbart, a veteran of sitcoms.

In this film, God (George Burns) taps an average earthling (John Denver) as His representative and, between all the comedic throwaways, instructs him to deliver a message that's about seventy-five per cent self-reliance and twenty-five per cent faith. This is probably the most ecumenical movie ever made. The God shown is an inoffensive TV God, not the character in Randy Newman's "God's Song" despite a similar thrust. To say that the film makes Unitarianism seem strident by comparison is almost an understatement.

Oh, God! also shows that Reiner's directing style is as deeply rooted in television as his writing style. The film is full of the tight little reaction shots that are so typical of TV dramas and seem so cheap on film. Also, the jokes are evenly spaced, as in a sitcom. The same points can be made about *The One And Only*, which suffers additionally from the general visual flatness of a movie-of-the-week and in fact actually looked taped, not filmed at all. The more important aspect of *The One And Only*, however, is this 1950s business, this harking back to a television ethos in more than a technical way. Here again, once presumes Reiner should by rights share screen credit, this time with Steve Gordon, another network script jockey.

Ostensibly the film is a vehicle for Henry Winkler, who seems determined to counter his nice guy TV image by playing asinine roles in films — first in *Heroes*, now in this one. Beneath that exploitative function, however, the film has another purpose. On this level it's a retelling of *Enter Laughing*, Reiner's autobiographical play which he later adapted for the screen. The storyline is basically that Winkler is a struggling, hustling young actor (the role should have been played by Richard Dreyfuss) who, after various setbacks, does not finally attain stardom, but gives up and becomes a crooked wrestler.

Now there are several little points here. Until *Oh, God!*, Reiner went through a period of striking cynicism, directing such films as *Where's Poppa?* and *The Comic*. Cynicism, implying as it does a certain awareness and experience, has never really had much of a television following. Reiner seemed bitter about television and was beginning to put the feeling to worthwhile use in such films. But when these didn't turn out to be big box-office movies, he traded artistic promise for commercial stability, just as Winkler's character does in this film. But Reiner's sellout is nowhere so complete as the wrestler's. The fact that this film is no *Next Stop, Greenwich Village*, in which talent wins out in the end over indifference and despair, is the main argument in favour of its integrity.

Enter Laughing, filmed in 1967, was Reiner's reminiscences of his own early days, the days before television made him a disconsolate name instead of a self-respecting nobody . . . the 1950s. *The One And Only* is set in the 1950s for absolutely no good reason except that wrestling was a staple of early television and has come to symbolise for Reiner its fraudulence. It's also the story of the young *Enter Laughing* hero (that is, Reiner himself) one step farther along towards justified cynicism. The main character in *The One And Only* is supposed to live in a world of nonstop cheap jokes, the sly self-sickening shtik of one who can deal with others only through quick insults and constant patter. Winkler, however, fails to perceive this and makes the character out to be uncomplicated smart-ass. Winkler is a television actor and doesn't understand much beyond finding his mark, saying his lines and radiating personality.

Reiner, conversely, is of the older generation, with a sensibility arising from the stage, and for him the film's failure must be bittersweet. Television has always been dominated by comedy because comedy is cheap to produce and easy to make palatable. If recently the trend has been towards topical comedy dressed as social criticism, this has meant only that now even TV's door has been closed to Reiner and some of his contemporaries. They can't escape the stigma of their televised pasts but neither can they quit the present and return. Reiner's friend Brooks, for instance, has become successful only by stalking the cult audience, by sending up the work of James Whale, Hitchcock and others. As such, he seems to pass for a filmmaker. But look at the work of his disciples, Gene Wilder and Marty Feldman. They didn't come up through the ranks of 1950s live New York television. They lack the manic desperation of a director with secrets to hide. The result is that their films look like the stupid television pap which Brooks, Reiner and others so hate but cannot help retain traces of. The lesson here, I suppose, is that television is a reactive medium. One produces usable work by fighting against it. The alternative is to let one's mind become an all-night doughnut shop.

April 1978

Candice Bergen: Art, Artifice, Dentrifice

Film criticism is a much more recent cultural force than film itself, particularly in North America. It's only in the past fifteen years that we've had more than a small handful of major critics writing regularly at one time, analysing the same films, directors and actors simultaneously. Much of the present excitement in film criticism comes from the fact that we can choose from, and compare, critics with dissimilar backgrounds and entirely different aesthetic, sociological and historical approaches. Against such diversity sparks are struck and with the sparks come fire. Still, there are some points of convergence among these writers, summary opinions common to them all, from which no one seems willing to break ranks and dispute. One of these opinions is that Candice Bergen is little more than a pretty face, a decoration; that she's an actress *manquée*, a sort of female Burt Reynolds only less a phenomenon and of no more social significance. This judgment, as I say, is rampant. It is also, I believe, wrong. In fairness it's not difficult to see how this canard come into being. What's puzzling is why no important critic has revised his or her view of Bergen who has gone through (by my count) three stages and changed much for the better.

Bergen is perhaps the most frequently damned actress of the time partly on some principle and partly because she also has been one of the most frequently miscast. In all but a couple of the dozen films she's made since her debut in 1966 she's either been put in roles completely contrary to her personality (though ones supposedly consistent with her appearance) or else in roles from which only a wizard could have salvaged anything at all. What's now come about is not so much an improvement in her acting as a triumph of her rightful disposition over foul scripts. This has been possible in part because the kind of woman she seems to be, or at least the kind she best portrays — a sort of Superwoman — has finally come into her own as a nonpareil. By contrast, her two previous specialties — the Ingenue and the Captive — were traditional casting department figures. She was not necessarily poorly suited to them; she was just no better suited to them than anyone else.

Her first film, Sidney Lumet's adaptation of Mary McCarthy's novel *The Group*, was made when she was nineteen years old. It caused her to be thought of as an Ingenue because of the nature of the character she played rather than because of the performance she gave, which is actually one of her most adept. Someone somewhere decided that she thenceforth would be the debutante, the snooty jetsetter, the young American woman who thinks she's the greatest thing since vaseline. In short, she was stereotyped as Bryn Mawr's legacy to the world, and it is an immutable law of stereotyping that each such performance is a little less substantial than the last. In Bergen's case the decline was especially rapid. The next year, 1967, she appeared in two Ingenue movies, *Vivre pour vivre* and *The Day the Fish Came Out*. The second of these speaks for all such films. It was a Greek production (with a score by Mikis Theodrakis) based on the incident in which the U.S. Air Force jettisoned two atomic bombs off the coast of Spain. It was a comedy, and Bergen's devoir was to walk along a desolate beach looking blonde and wearing a sort of abbreviated spacesuit. There were Ingenue elements in some of her later films as well, notably Mike Nichols' *Carnal Knowledge* and Richard Rush's *Getting Straight*, though by that time, 1970, she was well into being a Captive instead.

In crass movie terms, the difference between the Ingenue and the

110

Captive is mainly a difference in the kinds of sexual fantasies they generate. The Ingenue is more the girl from the next class than the girl next door whereas the Captive is a more accessible fantasy figure by being a more nebulous one. Her position is ambiguous in the fantasiser's mind. He can leave her to her fate and watch the fireworks or else he can win her affection by rescuing her.

Bergen was a Captive by turns in Robert Wise's *The Sand Pebbles*, in which she was on the verge of being raped by Chinese revolutionaries; in Ralph Nelson's *Soldier Blue*, in which she was taken prisoner by warring Indians; and in her most recent film, John Milius' *The Wind and the Lion*, in which she's held hostage by a Berber chieftain. In each case, she is the good-looking Anglo-Saxon woman (in one instance a missionary, in another a wealthy widow) who's thrust into danger on foreign soil. Thus, she fulfills the audience's xenophobic nightmares as well as their vicarious wet-dreams. She has also been a Captive on a more sophisticated level. For instance, in *Carnal Knowledge* she was trapped in a bad marriage to Art Garfunkel and in Herbert Ross's *T.R. Baskin* she was trapped in the slums of Chicago, which are every bit as frightening as the Yangtse Valley in 1920. Both these films were made in 1971 when Bergen (so it now appears) was on her way to breaking free and becoming the Superwoman.

In a sense, her first role, as the cool intelligent lesbian of *The Group*, began as a Superwoman role, though this element of the characterisation was forced into the background by the competing Ingenue as the story moved forward; such cinematic sibling rivalry is present in some of her later films as well, up to and including *The Wind and the Lion*. For instance, the film *11 Harrowhouse*, released last year, showed her as both Ingenue and Superwoman, though the two stances assumed proportions opposite to the ones exhibited in *The Group*. In this more recent film, she was ostensibly an Ingenue of great beauty and coyness, a Cybill Shepherd sort of character. But she also a neo-Nietzschenne who masterminded a diamond robbery which she then executed with Charles Grodin, who by comparison seemed weak and mealy mouthed.

The robbery was planned and carried out, one felt, not as an act of avarice or as a social or political gesture but rather as proof of her self-assurance and individuality in an age of mediocrity and tyrannical conformity. It marked a change in her career not because it showed how undistinguished she was when she was trying to act (we already knew this from watching and reading) but because

111

it showed how accomplished her acting is when she is being natural. The superficiality of the character didn't work very well, though the director wisely made use of it for comic effect. What worked beautifully was her determination and intelligence, her freedom devoid of arrogance. This marked the emergence of the Superwoman and, finally, the beginning of the end for the Ingenue and the Captive.

The two films Bergen has appeared in since then — *The Wind and the Lion* and *Bite the Bullet*, both in current release — carry this characterisation still further. In the first of these, a farfetched historical action film, she portrays Mrs Pedecaris, a character out of a three-decker novel. She's the widow of a British diplomat living in North Africa who's held a political hostage by Raisuli, "the last of the Barbary pirates," played rather ludicrously by Sean Connery. It's an unimportant film in every way except for Bergen's character.

Her strong-willed Mrs Pedecaris is equal parts of the present-day free spirit everyone is striving to emulate and of her almost Shavian antecedent who went through life quite epigrammatically, thank you, with everything perfectly under control. In fact, *The Wind and the Lion* bears a striking resemblance to *Captain Brassbound's Conversion* in basic outline and in the way the woman's self-assurance and independence and complete lack of pretension make her male opposite number seem ineffectual. As Shaw's Lady Cicely Waynflete did in the case of Brassbound, Bergen's Pedecaris makes Raisuli look silly what with his abstract notions of glory and his nonpragmatic interest in war. The comparison is not so farfetched as it may sound. If Shaw were writing today, he would be writing for Candice Bergen rather than Ellen Terry, and one cannot escape the speculation that they would alter one another for the better. Bergen's other new film, *Bite the Bullet*, an adventure comedy co-starring Gene Hackman and James Coburn and written and directed by Richard Brooks, involves much the same sort of character. Here she is less clearly delineated, however, by reason of being less central to the story, which turns on a mounted race across the American west in 1906. Still, the basic ingredients are present. Together the two films show that Bergen could well assume, in this age of the female, a position as important to popular culture as Bogart occupied in the wartorn age of the male.

Pauline Kael, one of Bergen's harshest accusers but probably the most reliable critic of film-acting writing today, has called Bergen "a movie star by act of nature." This refers to her physical attractiveness, and also perhaps to her famous father Edgar Bergen, though I myself have never understood the nepotistic link between the two careers that's sometimes alleged to exist. At any event, she is in fact a movie star in the general sense of the phrase but much different from earlier ones. Historically, the function of the movie star has been, in times of prosperity, to divert our attention from the world by entertaining us and, in times of upheaval, to entertain us by diverting our attention. Bergen's place (perhaps this is true of a few other actors as well) is different. It's to entertain without diverting but rather by focusing attention on herself — on what women and by extension all of us could be: responsible first to ourselves alone and only then being all things to all people, as some of Shaw's characters were. Her task is to be an exemplar without being an ideal. As Bergen the Superwoman, she's succeeded nicely.

First take her appearance and her carriage. Movie stars of the past came in two varieties. There were the glamorous ones who all looked pretty much alike. Then there were the individualistic ones (like Bogart, they usually rose through the ranks as character actors) who looked like no one else at all. The former were unrealistic at a basic level, and while they were entertaining they ultimately suffered from overfamiliarity as a type. We knew, for instance, that no one in real life ever really looked like Jean Harlow (let alone behaved like her), or that if anyone did, it was only because that person was doing an imitation. The latter kind of star didn't resemble their colleagues so much, even though they were quite as homely as the Harlows were gorgeous, and they were unrealistic on another plane. We believed that the rugged types existed, mainly on the fringes of society. But we knew that nowhere, not even in Casablanca, was there really anyone resembling Bogart, with a mug like a relief map yet such perfect teeth.

Bergen is different. She has one of those faces that never looks the same in any two photographs and that runs the gamut of resemblance from a magazine cover to a Mexican painting of Christ. What's more, she has an endearing way of pursing her lips in appreciation of someone else's (usually her male lead's) occasional flickers of independence, which promise but never quite match her own. She also has a habit of pulling strands of hair away from her face and of opening her eyes full wide in rapt attention. All this has the effect neither of diverting nor entertaining but of

113

making one think, yes, it is conceivable to meet such a person in life. Such meetings never actually take place, of course, but still, it is conceivable. Hope keeps one alive. More importantly, she projects enplus. This is a word I've just learned from a stray copy of *Vogue*, which I believe can be defined as a combination of non-kinetic energy and freedom of spirit.

And then there's her use of dialogue. Stanley Kaufmann of *The New Republic*, so far as I can determine, has only once conde-scended to mention Bergen's acting and that was to state "that she has never spoken a believable word on the screen." It's true that some of her lesser films displayed an awkwardness unrelated to any awkwardness apparently called for in the writing, but this too has been eliminated almost completely. Or rather, Bergen has reconciled this seeming lack of theatrical skill with her shift toward the Superwoman. In *11 Harrowhouse* she spoke to Grodin in tones of elated charlatanism, exactly the way such a character would speak in life. Her dialogue would have worked in the film even if the lines had been gibberish. Similarly, in *The Wind and the Lion* she speaks to Raisuli as though instructing a wayward child, not reprimanding or cajoling, but simply denying his power over her. She is asserting her superior equality, if you will, in everything but circumstance. This is just as it should be in a sense, since, thanks more to her performance than to the storyline, she is less a Captive than he is, though she alone is a prisoner.

In neither of these films, then, can one believe that Bergen is play-ing other than herself. The effect is created partly by the way she carries herself and the way she speaks. One is reminded of the old-fashioned literary dictum about the best short stories being those which commence with the beginning of the action and conclude with the finish of it, yet which give the reader an indication of what has taken place before and what will take place afterward. Bergen's most remarkable acting is like this. One has a sense that the lines being uttered off-camera are equal to those we actually hear on the screen.

John Simon, who finds films generally in poor taste but who at least has fun writing about them, once remarked that Bergen's "pseudoacting continues not to improve," and many lesser critics have all but made second careers out of running her to ground. In the end, it is Kael who's the most perceptive of the lot. Her alter-nating damnation and backhanded encouragement mark her as the only one who seems on the verge of identifying Bergen's progress. She first wrote, in the course of discussing something else, that Bergen "suggested some bright possibilities as a comedian." Later she withdrew this with a terse comment, ". . . she's no actress." Later still she came around to admitting, in another aside, that Bergen "gives evidence of intelligence and humor in print and on television" whatever she does in films.

That last remark may well prove an important one, for what, in the final analysis, Bergen is becoming is a sort of public-woman, somewhat akin to the old man-of-letters who acts as both social yardstick and artist by maintaining in a variety of public media a position consistent with the one maintained privately.

September 1975

Peering over the
Dotted Line

I

By Christmas time, *Janis*, a film about
(in order of importance) the music
and the personality of Janis Joplin,
will have opened in Canada, where it
was made. As perhaps the most
thoughtful rock documentary to date,
it is almost assured pleasant notices
and attentive audiences. But by that
time the movie's farther-reaching
commercial importance may have
been confirmed in the U.S., where it
will already have been in release
some two months.

Janis is an emotionally appealing
but non-sensational study of the leading white blues singer of her generation and it bears no trace of the dis-
cord and hassle from which it
emerged. The man who put it
together by (uncharacteristically for a
Canadian) piling gamble upon gamble, is a sixty-two-year-old veteran
named Frank (Budge) Crawley. He
feels that the film, following the
current success of the Canadian-

made *Apprenticeship of Duddy Kravitz*, will leave in Los Angeles and elsewhere the impression "that maybe those Canadians can do something right after all." This realisation struck him, he says, during his negotiations with Universal, who will distribute the picture worldwide except for Canada. "After three weeks of talks," he remembers, "they were still calling me Budge Baby, and they only call you Budge Baby when it's going to make money."

The story of the making of *Janis* is one of those incredibly complicated yarns in which it frequently appears as though everyone involved is about to litigate against everyone else. It began four years ago with Festival Express '70, a government-sponsored troupe of performers who were to travel by train across much of the country giving concerts. The original plan called for them to begin in Montreal, but Mayor Jean Drapeau shut them out of his city because of the FLQ crisis. Instead, they began in Toronto and worked their way as far as Calgary. The cast included Joplin, the Band, the Grateful Dead, and Ian and Sylvia. This scheme prompted a Toronto entrepreneur to organise a company called Festival Express Productions for the purpose of tagging along on the train to make a film. The entrepreneur was Willem Poolman, a lawyer who had never made a film before but had been involved in the Canadian movie world as a 16mm distributor. Poolman talked Design Craft, a part of the mammoth Maclean-Hunter communications complex, into a contract for shooting. Other partners included Kenny Walker and the two department store heirs, Thor and George Eaton. Mind you, this and what follows is the barest outline.

By the time the train was in Winnipeg, the production company had run out of money. It had $35,000 in debts including a $15,000 debt to Maclean-Hunter for sound recording, and legal fees would eventually total another thirty-five gees. "The Eatons threw Poolman out a couple of times," recalls Crawley who became a secondary creditor by lending money to one of the primary ones. "The whole thing was very confused." The equipment house hadn't been paid. Neither had the lab nor the three cameramen, one of whom had worked on *Woodstock*, and another of whom, left staring at a hundred thousand feet of film, removed himself and the Joplin footage home to England for a while. The film had yet to be processed, and at least one lab refused to touch it for fear of possible legal complications. The result was that the public receiver stored it in a Jack Frost food locker where it remained for three years. In the meantime, of course, Joplin had died from what was ruled an accidental heroin overdose. In the meantime, also, Budge Crawley had taken another financial gamble.

In Canadian terms, Crawley is one of the pioneers. An accountant by training, he is a big barrel-chested man with a face like that of Walter Huston in *The Treasure of Sierra Madre*, further enhanced by Sam Ervin eyebrows. His company began in 1931 when he started shooting an industrial film for free, just to get the experience, and processing it at night in his bathtub. It is now a prosperous film production and distribution operation with offices in Ottawa and Toronto, and the list of "sponsored" films it has turned out fills nearly ten columns of the entry for Crawley in one biographical dictionary. Crawley has a well earned reputation as one of the Canadian film industry's sharpest and least malicious producers and as the one most willing to take risks. This last side of him manifests itself at a creditors' meeting when he offered to put up the money, to a limit of $40,000, to print and sync the film and see what was there. What was there, he recalls, "was some pretty good stuff of Janis and the Band, both of whom were Albert Grossman artists." There was, in all, between ten thousand and fifteen thousand feet of the two acts. Crawley got control of the footage and Grossman, accompanied by Robbie Robertson of the Band, came up to screen it. The Band decided they could do better making a film about themselves alone and declined to grant the necessary licence. The project, which at some earlier point had been envisioned by someone as a Joplin movie, had now become that for certain, partly by default.

Already heavily committed financially, Crawley had no choice but to keep taking fliers. The next stop was the Janis Joplin estate, whose executrix was Janis's mother Dorothy Joplin. He flew to Port Arthur, Texas, where he screened the film for her and her lawyer. Fifty other filmmakers, he learned, had already made approaches and had been turned down, and the day after the singer's death some of them had even registered titles such as "Janis Joplin" and "The Janis Joplin Story" with the Motion Picture Producers' Association. At this writing another Joplin film, a fictionalised biography, is said to be in the works but bogged down in disputes about friends of the singer who are still alive.

At first, Crawley says, Dorothy Joplin was cautious and difficult. After seeing the film, however, both she and her counsel were moved. The mother said: "If you can make a film that's about what

Janis meant to her fans and I pass muster on it, go ahead. But if I
don't like it ..." One would guess this is also the type of self-protec-
tive deal she made with Myra Friedman, the author of the most
valuable Joplin book, *Buried Alive*, in which Mother Joplin is
treated gently. Crawley went ahead on spec. Gamble number
three, the big one.

The word went out for other Joplin footage, and Crawley des-
cribes the result as having been "a Fellini kind of scene" with
lawyers scurrying back and forth across the Atlantic with documents in several languages in an attempt to secure the necessary
permissions. The rights were acquired to the Joplin stuff from
Monterey Pop — and this is the only piece in the ninety-seven
minutes of final product previously seen in theatres (there is also
a scene from the Woodstock festival). A great source of new
material was the press coverage of Janis's 1969 European tour. Film
was procured from Bavaria Films in Munich and from other out-
fits in London, Frankfurt, Paris, Stockholm and elsewhere, not all
of it equal in quality or even under normal circumstances usable.
For instance, there was some fine audio stuff from Swedish state
radio and some nice video from someplace else that was only
recorded in mono. KQED, the San Francisco educational station,
turned up her first television appearance, and Crawley got releases
for both of her Dick Cavett interviews. In brief, the film came from
many sources, some obscure, and there were several near-misses.
A member of the late Big Brother group claimed to have some 8mm
stuff of Janis taken at a tattoo party, but a later ransacking of his
San Francisco apartment failed to produce it.

In the end the original Festival Express footage still comprised
over twenty per cent of the film. Despite this and the Canadian-
ness of the whole behind-the-scenes production, the Canadian
Film Development Corporation dragged its feet when approached
to make its usual arrangements. At length the CFDC did offer to
put in $80,000 but this was too little too late. At one time the Joplin
estate talked of helping to capitalise the project but the funds never
materialised. So it was Crawley who financed it with bank loans
that at one stage meant he was paying $8,000 a month interest,
which in Toronto represents a number of big movie loans indeed.

Much of the capital went toward rights and permissions.
Crawley had Janis performing eighteen of her songs on film and
each had to be cleared individually and painstakingly. As the
singer didn't write much of her own material, there wasn't much

119

the estate could help expedite. On the other songs the costs varied considerably. While most cost far less, the copyright clearances on "Summertime" (held by the Gershwin brothers) and "Me and Bobby McGee" (held by Kris Kristofferson) came to $5,000 each. The total was something upwards of $175,000 including the rights to show the performances, which required a great deal of detective work. Written into the budget are out-of-court settlements in the event of action by (for instance) a young woman shown climbing a West German stage and dancing with Janis. All efforts to identify her and secure her permission beforehand were unsuccessful.

To edit the film into an acceptable whole, Crawley hired and moved from the States to Ottawa Harold Alk, the former Pennebaker cameraman who directed *The Murder of Fred Hampton* and co-directed *Eat That Document*, an ABC special on Dylan and the Band. His role was really more than that of an editor; more like that of a post-mortem director or perhaps orchestrator. His work was not only artistically sound but, more vitally important in the production sense, sound in the eyes of Mrs Joplin. Crawley showed her a rough cut one year after their initial talk and she approved. Another gamble won.

Janis contains no mention of the singer's death and nothing of her personal life except what is directly connected with her music. There are no references to dope or sex. There is some pretty rough language, but oddly Mrs Joplin didn't object. Quite the opposite. In Canada the film is rated the equivalent of PG, but in the U.S. it's R because of the word fuck, which Dorothy Joplin refused to cut.

Alk faced some problems in preparing a feature documentary of the type needed from a shelf-full of film cans, and his solutions are entirely unobtrusive in the finished movie. For example, there was no film available of Janis doing her best known song "Me and Bobby McGee" except one bad performance when she was drunk on the train. So Alk ended the pastiche abruptly and used an audio of the song with acoustic guitar over a montage of her face. The suddenness of it seems to remind the audience of the suddenness of her death, and the lyrics of the song sum up a great deal of what we know of her personality. To balance this, he repeated the tactic at the beginning. Here he used her "Mercedes Benz" with stills of Janis and her famous kandy-kolored car, and others of the vehicle (owned by Grossman) sitting untended in a garage: another subtle statement on her demise. But Alk's real challenge was to show, without offending the Joplin estate, how singing the blues was as

120

natural an activity to Janis as burgling was for Richard Nixon. The result is that the film is not, like the Hendrix film, an autopsy laced with interviews with acquaintances and admirers and with scenes from the subject's years of anonymity; for one thing, in *Janis* the singer is performing ninety per cent of the time. Rather, it's a film specifically about the ontology of her songs and their roots in her past. In this, it is quite successful, and it will be curious to see how the Joplin biopic, if it actually gets made and released, will treat the same material.

Joplin's importance is that pervading everything she sang was the feeling that she meant it, and meaning the blues is the opposite of being cool. When she sang, she sweated and got red in the face and sounded completely autobiographical. Neither was she into flash (her tackiness was too authentic and she herself too mortal) or flash's predecessor, old fashioned show biz glamour. She tells an interviewer in the film: "I'm not wearing cardboard eyelashes and wearing girdles and playing in Las Vegas." She was a habitual loser who became famous for that without trying, but merely by attempting to get it out of her system. This comes through in all the *Janis* music and at several points in the interviews and informal conversation. Once it happens in an aside when she recalls having been a waitress in a bowling alley back in Texas ("two Schlitz and an order of french fries"). Another time it arises is in the Cavett sequence.

In the end the only Cavett material used was a clip of her performance on the show and her subsequent interview alone with him, when she tells of her plans to attend her high school class tenth reunion for the purpose of rubbing her classmates' noses in the memory of the shabby way they treated her. Following this are shots of the actual reunion in which she's interviewed by the Port Arthur media while her kid sister, still stuck there, looks on. It's more sad than bitter, like the story of her life, and like the whole film. In a number of sequences — the one with Cavett and others where she's on stage — she talks more than sings, often with a smart-ass alternate culture inarticulateness, which rings hollow. Alk seems to have included these to teach us how to see through them to the underlying despair she often sought to bury when not performing. Joplin, like most everyone else, was best when most sincere, and *Janis* is the same way.

Take One, November 1974

II

When an American president dies, no matter what kind of president he was, there are two things that can begin to happen to him in the public mind. He can be made an object of reverence, like Washington or Lincoln, or he can be made into a character, like Theodore Roosevelt or Andrew Jackson. No president is ever really forgotten about, the way some Canadian prime ministers are. Even the obscure ones, such as Millard Fillmore or Franklin Pierce, are rendered into caricatures by the fact of their obscurity; their names become amusing in a way the names of Sir John Abbott or Sir Mackenzie Bowell do not. What has happened frequently, at least in this century, is that a dead president has begun his afterlife as both a deity and a clown simultaneously, and that, as history has been written and as fashions have changed, one element has begun to eclipse the other. Kennedy, for instance, is right now slipping rapidly from canonisation as a saint to enshrinement as a lovable rogue. This process is often recorded in films. *Brother Can You Spare a Dime?* and *Give 'Em Hell, Harry* are two examples.

The first of these films was "written and directed" by Phillipe Mora. That is to say it was pieced together by him from archival and stock footage since there's no directing involved and practically no writing. It is ostensibly a nostalgia movie of the type *That's Entertainment* is beginning to make popular again, though it aims at something higher. It aims at being a portrait of the American 1930s in terms of social history; at least that's the way it is sold to the audience. What it seems to be for Mora himself, who is French, is less a documentary than a salute to a certain mythology. This is understandable enough in view of the attraction Americanness and Americanisms have always held for individual Frenchmen rather than for the official French public.

Mora is a filmmaker first and so not above including the extraneous simply because it is entertaining and unusual: the opening and closing sequences of a child reciting the list of forty-eight states in one breath, or the dirigible *Hindenberg* meandering over the Empire State Building. Such a casual attitude nearly destroys whatever value his film could have as a history lesson. He is so sloppy on chronology that relying on *Brother Can You Spare a Dime?* alone one would be unable to say whether Hoover succeeded Roosevelt or the other way around. There is only a skeleton of fact. What there is instead is a fawning tribute to the clichés of the 1930s

(I don't mean that in a derogatory way), the greatest of which is FDR. If Mora can call himself the writer and director of this film then it is not unreasonable to call Roosevelt the star.

The film is full of curious juxtapositions that are historically revealing almost in spite of themselves. For instance, there is a small bit of footage of Irving Thalberg and other representatives of real life Hollywood and a very great deal more from the imaginative Hollywood — the two turn out to be practically interchangeable. There are also quite a few clips from 1930s films showing Jimmy Cagney as a 1920s gangster (a nostalgia film within a nostalgia film). One of these is intercut with a Roosevelt speech. It is at this point that Mora hits upon an interesting mythological distinction, intentionally or otherwise. Cagney was a black hero: a man people enjoyed because he was so bad, a surrogate for danger. Roosevelt, conversely, was a white hero, to whom people turned, expectant, imploringly, when actual danger came sweeping into their lives. They expected him to be good. He was a surrogate Moses with a touch of the local bank manager to bring him into focus. Do what they will with a dead Moses, the people will always treat reverently rather than comically the shade of a bank manager, at least for a couple of generations.

Harry Truman was a different sort, with a different sort of cinematic afterlife. So far this afterlife consists of James Whitmore's portrayal in *Give 'Em Hell, Harry*, a filmed stage performance of the one-man play by Samuel Gallu. But this characterisation is actually part of a whole new attitude towards presidency in general, and owes more to wishful thinking and hope than to mere nostalgia. The film is enthralling for two reasons. The first is that Whitmore gives one of those loud, unsubtle performances which make you think he was born for the role (one-man shows are often like this when they're cooking). He has no competition and doesn't have to act except in the broadest possible gestures. Since his subject was a man with a strong theatrical streak, Whitmore is only copying the performance of the original, just as he did several years ago in the case of Will Rogers. The second reason the show works is that it says things the audience is dying to hear said. Truman was a populist but not a dummy. He knew he was best suited to the populist stance and he played it for all it was worth, which was a great deal indeed. Populists are just what the phrase implies: they appeal to the lowest common denominator. As a marketing principle that is good anytime; it is especially effective in moments of anxiety, before the actual crisis begins.

When the people were anxious about abolition they cried, "If only we had a man like Jackson." When they were anxious about the problems accompanying industrial expansion they cried, "If only we had a man like Lincoln." Diefenbaker, our only truly populist PM, is also the only one remembered in this way; it is a universal truth that populism induces memories. The poor have great faith in their own before the deluge. But once the deluge comes they prefer an aristocrat like Franklin Roosevelt with an authoritarian bearing rather than cornbelt philosophy. Right now is such a time. This is probably why, for instance, Theodore Roosevelt was depicted so lovingly in *The Wind and the Lion*. More noticeably, this is why *Give 'Em Hell, Harry* can be so rewarding if the viewer allows himself or herself to go along with the consensus of the mob. America is now in the curious position of finding a nice guy succeeding a bastard in the White House and of realising that being the Henry Fonda of politics is not sufficient in itself. In this stylised representation of Truman, however, America finds a ready made ideal: a nice guy who seemed sufficiently bastardly to appear effective; a man perfectly suited to the present however much a dangerous joke he was in the past.

Whitmore opens with Truman writing a letter in the Oval Office and pasting on the envelope his own personal postage stamp, bought and paid for with three cents from his own pocket. A cheer goes up from the audience on the soundtrack. Later he speaks of kicking a few asses in labour and in government and there is another round of applause. Here is profanity used not as Nixon used it, to express contempt and venality, but to mask the speaker's limited vocabulary. Many find this wonderful stuff. When Whitmore as Truman keeps talking of the "gubment" — in contradistinction to himself; he believed the two were separate — a glow spreads across audiences that could bring down the house. Or rather, the house seems to surrender in awe, as though to St Peter, that great civil servant in the sky.

What is implied without being stated is that Truman was an anachronism in the context of both the executive mansion and his own time. He was a Kansas City haberdasher caught up in ward politics on a grander scale than he'd ever known before. He called his elders sir because he still believed in a way that they were also his superiors. He was a character out of the 1920s, and it seemed at the time that his sins were more of omission than of commission.

The fact that he was a war criminal because he ordered the bombs on Hiroshima and Nagasaki has somehow come down to us as less true than the fact that he was *not* a war criminal because his side won.

December 1975 – January 1976

III

It must be said at the outset that Gregory Peck is first rate in the title role of Joseph Sergent's film *MacArthur*. He gives an amazingly vivid impression of Douglas MacArthur's appearance, bearing and way of speaking. More importantly, he has some success in his struggle to animate both the general's formal persona and his manner when in repose — two states which, for all we can learn, were in truth not very dissimilar. In short, Peck once or twice almost makes us forget that he is an actor playing a part — a cliché, I know, but one that's dangerous not because it's used too often but because it's so seldom true. With Hal Barwood and Matthew Robbins' script he does the neatest job imaginable considering that he is, after all, Gregory Peck.

This last remark is not facetious, for Peck, as luck would have it, came along in the 1940s, when nobody was any longer certain exactly what being an actor entailed. He came to attention at a time when an older breed, exemplified by John Barrymore, was dying off, the fashion having predeceased them. The day was gone, then, when actors were supposed to be agile impersonators imbuing everything they did with a deliberately theatrical quality. But if Peck missed the porcine era when the High Style overcompensated for what had been the actor's low estate, he also missed the true age of the movie star. By the war years, movie stars in the strict sense were obsolete; or at least, the back lots were by then a closed shop. People like Gable and Cooper knew only one stance, and the studios were continuing to churn out films designed for its display. Anti-trust suits had begun and television was just around the corner when Peck emerged in Hollywood. Until his time, stars were hatched within the big studios; afterwards, they often came from other branches of entertainment to be served by Hollywood. Peck was stuck in the middle, in a way he must have found unfortunate.

Had he come around just ten years earlier, with his smooth black hair and ninety-degree jaw, Peck would have been typecast, but on a high level, as the bridegroom's handsome friend, a sort of Ronald Reagan with depth. As it was, with the studios crumbling, he played such characters but in starring rather than supporting roles. He became famous for portraying, not charismatic types or adventurers or lovers or scoundrels, but nice guys. For many years, in fact, he has been the quintessential nice guy of film. By comparison, even Henry Fonda has more often been the villain. Peck's appropriateness to this distinction was aided by the fact that his acting and his personality were in harmony. On screen, he discredited anti-Semitism in *Gentleman's Agreement* and the advertising business in *The Man in the Gray Flannel Suit*. Off screen, he campaigned for various liberal politicians and produced *The Trial of the Catonsville Nine*. All this makes his work here more interesting because Douglas MacArthur was anything but a nice guy.

It has been widely reported that George C. Scott was originally asked to play the part. Wisely, he declined. He already had taken a shot at this sort of personality a few years back in Franklin J. Schaffner's *Patton*. Once such part is acting, two is politics. And the politics of *MacArthur*, sorry to say, are even more offensive than those of the other film and just as obvious as the inescapable comparison. In *Patton*, there was a brief scene during a battle in which two soldiers, real Ernie Pyle types, had the following exchange as Patton rode by. "There goes Old Blood and Guts," said the first. "Yeah," the second replied. "*Our* blood and guts." There is a similar bit in *MacArthur* in which one Bill Mauldin stereotype comments admiringly, sardonically, to the other Bill Mauldin stereotype as the general just happens to pass by. This and more important resemblances can perhaps be explained by the fact that both films were produced by Frank McCarthy, himself a retired general, who appears to have had unusually strong artistic control.

MacArthur shows the subject during the Second World War and the Korean War, with only a few hints at his earlier career and a few scenes from later life, such as the famous "old soldiers" speech. This is both too bad and sinister. Depicting mainly MacArthur's Pacific exploits and his dismissal will leave naïve youth to conclude that, however uppity, MacArthur was merely a great wartime hero who was wrongly sacked during a period of relative peace. The truth, of course, is that he was an egotistical, dangerous, unstable crackpot who should not have been given command of a half dozen copyboys and who was much more a threat to his country than many of the enemies he quashed. This should be qualified only to the extent that he can be placed in the context of some of the other bloodthirsty lunatics who were his compatriots.

The America MacArthur loved was an abstract, for he lived abroad mostly or at West Point, which is a world unto itself. His father won a Congressional Medal of Honor at age seventeen in the Civil War and, by the time of his son's birth, was chasing across the southwest some of the last remaining free native peoples, who were understandably cross. MacArthur was a cavalry post brat. He was part of what became an entire generation of American generals with familial links to the days of frontier slaughter. MacArthur, though, rose through the ranks more quickly than the others. He was already a four-star general and the chief of staff in Washington, for instance, when Patton and Eisenhower were majors and George C. Marshall a colonel. He attained such a station, however, in a time of damnable peace. To occupy his mind, he disregarded the orders of Hoover (the first of the presidents he crossed) and used infantry, cavalry, machine guns and tanks on unarmed veterans during the Depression, as well as on a crowd of even more innocent bystanders on Pennsylvania Avenue. This "campaign," during which men and women were shot and bayonetted and infants killed in a gas attack, was also notable in another way. It marked the occasion on which Patton, gleefully following MacArthur's orders, used sabres against a defenceless man who had been decorated for saving his, Patton's, life fifteen years earlier in France. *MacArthur* does not deal at all with these and other sordid episodes.

Oh attempts are made to show the general's ego, his use of such famous props as the walking stick and the corncob pipe, his political ambitions and his way with the press. But such touches are largely confined to one section of the film, as though to jazz it up between battle scenes. We do not see the MacArthur who installed fifteen-foot mirrors in his office so as never to be out of his own sight and who always spoke of himself in the third person, with dramatic emphasis. Neither, more significantly, do we get the full impact of his always wanting to go to war — with anyone, almost — to satisfy his own glory-hunger and justify the existence of himself and others like him.

Eisenhower, often spoken of but never seen, comes across in a kindly light if only because of MacArthur's contempt for him; and this is not a bad way to remember him — the Eisenhower who, when himself a dying old general, tried to tell people that a real war in Vietnam would be a mistake if only on military grounds, the only ones he knew. There are also some good scenes of Mac-Arthur with Truman, played well in the James Whitmore manner by Ed Flanders, and Roosevelt (who is harder to mimic in a sense) played not badly by Dan O'Herlihy, the old Irish character actor. But nowhere does the film fulfil its moral obligation of emphasizing, even by negative example, that generals ought to be created in the unfortunate event of war, not the other way around. No one will find much fault with Peck's execution of this role: he uses all his emotional equipment to be ruthless and off-balance while seeming calm. One can question only his willingness to accept it. Perhaps it is simply that, at sixty-one, he wanted to have a final go at a solid part and finish in one great consummation of self-satisfaction. But that's the way MacArthur felt about the Third World War.

October 1977

128

IV

Los Angeles County has seven million people, of whom one million are on welfare and at least another million, maybe two, are illegal Mexican aliens whom everyone else exploits. It also has five million automobiles. Perhaps as many as a dozen of these are taxis, but they seem to operate only on weekends. It is also full of curious religious groups, doughnut stands, kosher Mexican junk food places run by Japanese, and wealthy middle-aged orthodontists, each with an ounce of cocaine in his glove compartment. Alan Rudolph's first film, *Welcome to L.A.*, purports to be an impressionistic study of the effects of this environment on individuals and couples. It fails. Rudolph is school of Altman (the film in fact is produced by Altman). The result is that terribly boring, one-dimensional characters go about mumbling snappy dialogue beneath heavy eyelids. Geraldine Chaplin to her husband Harvey Keitel: "People change." Harvey Keitel to his wife Geraldine Chaplin: "Not even the weather changes here." The film has a fine cast, including Sally Kellerman, Sissy Spacek and Lauren Hutton, and a useful score, by Richard Baskin, of the kind one associates with Altman films. But it also displays all the master's faults. Such as the failure to reconcile loose ends with a tight, swooping structure and the tendency to tell too many stories at once at the expense of telling any particular one meaningfully.

December 1977 – January 1978

V

When Nathanael West was writing his last novella *The Day of the Locust* in 1939 he set some of the action at a place he called National Films. The fictional studio was a composite of Columbia Pictures, where he had begun work as a screenwriter four years earlier, and Paramount Pictures, where he had many friends, including his brother-in-law S.J. Perleman. But in John Schlesinger's film version of *The Day of the Locust*, this action takes place at Paramount, for this is a Paramount release. The reversion of name is studio breastbeating of course but it is also a sign that West is not hated and reviled by Hollywood, as he no doubt would have liked to be, but rather esteemed as part of the film industry's supposedly glorious history. It is sad in a way that West, who died the year after the book was published, did not live to see this sign of approval. It is sad but also typical of him, for he was forever in the wrong place at the wrong time, posthumously as well as in life.

West is a writer with an enviable reputation for being neglected. He is also said to be a master of irony. Upon examination, however, the bitterest irony turns out to be in his life rather than in his four short works of fiction, for he was always too late or too early. Born in 1903, he missed the post-First World War bohemianism he would have enjoyed and even the better part of the excitement of the 1920s. He got to Paris during the finale, and while he edited with William Carlos Williams a little magazine, the revived *Contact*, this was in the early 1930s, after such periodicals had ceased to mean what they meant a few years earlier. He spent his entire career grasping at the tail ends of reputations and movements, and this applies to his film-life as well. He came to the business of movies after the great wave of cynical writers, recruited from the newspapers and the stage in silent days, had pretty well exhausted the subject of Hollywood as the Jerusalem of sham and cheap tinsel. There was little left for West to work with, though in *Locust* he certainly did what he could. But if he was born after his rightful time, he died before his second most rightful time began. He missed, poor man, his chance to be a Beat, a role in which he would have flourished, and his only other work to be filmed, a 1958 adaptation of *Miss Lonelyhearts* called simply *Lonelyhearts*, did nothing to revive or to straighten out his reputation.

Lonelyhearts should have been made in the 1960s, when its combination of pathos and cynicism would have been eaten up. *The*

Day of the Locust is the one that should have been filmed in 1958, when it would have seemed, if not fresh, then part of a cycle. As it is, it is at least to the good that *Locust* has been directed by Schlesinger, who understands or at least enjoys West because he seems, from his previous movies, to be much the same sort of character.

West, whose real name was Nathaniel von Wallenstein Weinstein, was the son of Russian immigrants to the Lower East Side of New York, and he clearly followed the pattern of behaviour of the first generation Americans of that time by wanting to be more American than it is really possible for anyone to be. He was the type of fellow who pursued Americanness with such dedication that he forgot that he was also a Jew, though likely he would have remembered, as so many others in his position did, had he lived to hear about the atrocities of the Second World War. At any rate, he was a classic example in American literature of the child-of-immigrants who relished everything indigenous even while being good-naturedly sardonic towards it. It is this sardonic attitude, mostly making fun of his subject but partly making fun of his own enthusiasm, that is often mistaken for black humour. *The Day of the Locust* film is a fortunate pooling of talent because Schlesinger, a respected veteran of the London stage, is the same type of immigrant West was. In fact, Schlesinger is the same type of Englishman that West was a Jew: one trying desperately to live down his heritage and masquerade his liking for apple pie, which would give him away were it revealed, by wallowing instead in supposed urbanity and cynicism. This attitude, or the trend towards it, has been the theme of Schlesinger's film career, from *Darling* in 1965, which he made while still in England paving the way; to *Midnight Cowboy* in 1969, which a native American would have made as either a documentary or a comedy; to *The Day of the Locust*, which was written with this director in mind but which Schlesinger, for all his good ideas, still manages to botch.

West's book is almost as misunderstood as Schlesinger's film is likely to become and for much the same reasons. The former is thought to be grotesque tale about Hollywood freaks. Part of the standard interpretation is that the dwarf Abe Kusich, with his physical deformity, points up the spiritual deformity of the other characters. A more sensible view is that West was striving to become a virtuoso by bringing new life to characters chosen deliberately for their familiarity as stereotypes. Schlesinger seems to

131

subscribe to both positions. On the one hand, he plays up the freakishness to a degree undreamt of in the text, till his production resembles a collaboration between Tod Browning and Otto Preminger. On the other, he becomes more a virtuoso than West ever was by casting actors who look exactly like the shallow stereotypes of the characters they portray, and then directing them with such style that they overcome this initial pigeonholing.

For example, Karen Black, in all her films, always has looked, as an actress and a human being, like a blonde starlet. Schlesinger casts her as Faye Greener, a character who is precisely that, giving her a base of believability below which she cannot fall, then luring her far above it to what is probably the most controlled acting she has ever done. Similarly, Donald Sutherland often has looked and talked like a lummox, so here, with short hair and an extra forty pounds, he plays Homer Simpson, the arch lummox of them all. In the same way, William Atherton plays Tod Hackett, the bland but potentially dissipated clean cut young man of talent, and Burgess Meredith plays Harry Greener, the broken-down vaude-villian. It's something of a brilliant stroke.

Still, in the direction of Schlesinger and in the script by Waldo Salt (who adapted *Midnight Cowboy*) there are many things to puz-zle. Some are tiny. For instance, why in the book did Harry Greener make his living selling silver polish in cans while on the screen he sells furniture polish in bottles? Others are medium-sized, such as: why is Claude Estee, a screenwriter in West's novella, a studio art director and hence Hackett's boss, and why are both men sudden-ly graduates of Yale? Still other points are large and raise real problems of interpretation. For example, why do Salt and Schle-singer tell and show us so little of "The Burning of Los Angeles," the painting that is to be Hackett's masterpiece, but make so much of the riot at the end of the story which is meant to be the proposed painting come to life? One could go on. Suffice it to say that this screen version is good source material for the study of fiction into film and also that Schlesinger, as though uncertain of himself in the immigrant manner, sticks closely to no one's idea of the book except his own, for better or for worse, probably worse.

Even as West was writing, Scott Fitzgerald was working on *The Last Tycoon* and Budd Schulberg on *What Makes Sammy Run?*, two vastly different writers who were nonetheless treating Hollywood as a big sad dream they both had experienced, a too-tempting place that had given them some fun perhaps but done them no good —

132

Faye Greener made manifest as a city and a circumstance. West would have liked to have written this way as well, but he was different. Like Fitzgerald he had come too late to know what it had really been like, but unlike Fitzgerald he never had been in the thick of anything and so had some difficulty imagining. He hid his inadequacy for the job under a cataclysmic vision of popular culture that he never really believed in.

The irony is that this gave him an immense popularity among the young of later generations, who did so believe, and each student to happen upon his work thought himself the first to rediscover it. The double irony is that Schlesinger's film, in the way adaptations of classics have of doing, will no doubt increase the audience for the book enormously while lessening greatly its impact and influence. Black humour has become far blacker than could ever have been imaged by West, who was born too late to see the decadents and died too soon to read Terry Southern and Mordecai Richler. Schlesinger is somewhat luckier. He and the spirit of Nathanael West are like to two cannibals stranded together in the wilds. The one has killed off the other to live to eat another day.

July 1975

133

VI

No one should be misled about *Eyes of Laura Mars*, directed by Irvin Kershner, being the sum of its parts. Like all the other memorable Kershner films (*The Hoodlum Priest, The Luck of Ginger Coffey, A Fine Madness, The Flim Flam Man*) the story is built upon the tension between two recognisable types. Between the urban people, who are sophisticated or canny or both, and the outcasts who are either more or less lovable, according to the demands of their opponents. Also, half the screenplay credit goes to David Zelag Goodman, who is acquiring a reputation for his work with city sleaze. Despite all this, the film bears the benchmark of only one person, the producer, Jon Peters. Like his other lavish production, *A Star is Born*, this is a film in which style is everything, in which the techniques of made-for-TV movies are fleshed out almost indefinitely by big budgets but without any proportional increase in substance.

Described in print, the film sounds like one that proceeded logically from a title instead of from an idea (which may well be the case remembering that the gambler in *The Big Sleep* was named Eddie Mars). Laura, another stylish, silently aggressive role for Faye Dunaway, is a New York photographer whose flair for the kinky has made her a minor media sensation. Her photographs of pasty-skinned kewpies in garter belts and positions of forced repose (the actual photos are by Helmut Newton and his imitator, Rebecca Blake) create an even bigger stir when it's discovered that they're almost blueprints for the scenes of several unsolved icepick murders. What's more, it becomes apparent that simultaneously with each crime Laura Mars has a vision of the victim dying, as though the killer were instantaneously projecting his field of vision into her mind. The psychic aspect of all this is practically taken for granted — leastwise never explained — and the final resolution of the mystery plot is wholly unsatisfactory.

The film's appeal rests instead in its mannered evocation of the new upper-middle-class bohemianism, which differs from previous varieties in several important ways. It constantly takes itself seriously, for one. And if rebellion plays very little part at all, penury plays absolutely none; the mood is in fact a spendthrift one without being in the least devil-may-care. There's a constant awareness of the past but it's informed neither by scholarship nor nostalgia — just something like numb regret, as though we are all picking through the ashes of some grander civilisation. The fact that this bohemianism is essentially apolitical is shown by the fact that, though its participants live and work exclusively in reclaimed industrial buildings and countinghouses and affect outdated notions of glamour, they're not mourning capitalism, or even acknowledging the irony. If grieving at all, they do so for New York, which they believe is dying and not simply continuing the urban life cycle, passing to Los Angeles the title of capital once yielded to it by Philadelphia and Boston. Such is the current mood of SoHo (which is often as not spelled Soho) where the Perrier flows like water and cocaine is the opium of the people. In its set direction, its wardrobe, its location work and its photography, *Laura Mars* captures it infinitely better than, say, Mazursky's *An Unmarried Woman* did. I suspect the preservation of this mood will in time give the film a documentary legitimacy.

October–November 1978

INDEX OF PERSONS AND TITLES